The Broken Parts of Us

The Broken Series

Ker Dukey

THE BROKEN PARTS OF US (The Broken)
Copyright © 2014 Ker Dukey
Published by Ker Dukey

All rights reserved. No part of this book may be reproduced or transmitted in any form, including electronic or mechanical, without written permission from the publisher, except in the case of brief quotations embodied in critical articles or reviews.

This is a work of fiction. Names, characters, businesses, places, events, and incidents are either the products of the author's imagination or used in a fictitious manner. Any resemblance to actual persons, living or dead, or actual events is purely coincidental.

This book is licensed for your personal enjoyment only. This book may not be re-sold or given away to other people. If you would like to share this book with another person, please purchase an additional copy for each person you share it with. If you are reading this book and did not purchase it, or it was not purchased for your use only, then you should return it to the seller and purchase your own copy. Thank you for respecting the author's work.

Published: Ker Dukey 2014
Publishing assisted by Black Firefly:
http://www.blackfirefly.com/
(Shedding light on your self-publishing journey)

BLACK FIREFLY

Editing: Kyra Lennon
Cover Design: Michelle Alexandme Designs
Proofreading: Chrystal
Formatting by: **http://www.blackfirefly.com/**

Dedication

To my readers -- thank you for coming back for another crazy ride. To everyone who has, or is looking for, that soul-consuming love. And to everyone who's heard the words "I could just devour you" and had their panties melt. They say love is powerful -- well, so is lust......

Prologue
Jasper

Danny's glare had solidified my insides; I couldn't move.

People assume if someone pulled a gun on them they would wrestle it away and use it against the person, or they would say a big "fuck you" and accept the bullet.

We're all fucking heroes in the "what if" game, but I can tell you, I am not a wimp. I can hold my own in a fight, I don't shy away from conflict, and I'll have my friends' backs any situation. But when a gun is pointed at you by a mad man, you revert back to being a little boy. Your body seizes, fear holds you hostage, your life flashes before your eyes, and you start praying that you'll get to see the people you love again, even if there are only two of them.

I might be a happy-go-lucky man whore, but I'm still a person. I have wants and ambitions. I don't want to die for no other reason than someone going off the deep end. I want to live, experience life.

You run scenarios through your head; maybe if I kicked his legs out from under him? Maybe if I try to communicate with him? Maybe if I beg? But for me, my body wouldn't comply with any of these things. I was in shock! My best friend's girl, my friend, River, held her dead brother – a man I had shared beers with—and her crazy ass boyfriend who fucking hated me was talking about River and me like we were an item while holding a gun on me.

······*Then he shot me*······

So every person that says they would do this or that, live in my motherfucking shoes. You don't know what you would do, or how it'll change you until you're looking down the barrel of a gun with a crazy motherfucker holding the trigger.

Jasper

I hear River's screams. They're deafening and I can't reach her. I'm paralyzed to the spot; blood seeps from me, covering the shirt I'm wearing.

Danny's eyes penetrate mine; they're so dark and cold. I look over at River. She's cracking like she's made of clay; pieces come away as her mouth screams. Blaydon is at her feet; he sits up. He's pale grey in colour, his eyes glossed over with an icy sheen, and his mouth is open, talking to me. I can't understand what he's saying.

"I can't hear you!" I shout to him.

"Wake up, Jasper. Come on, you're okay, you're okay. Wake up."

I gasp for air as my eyes open and adjust to the surroundings. Strong arms are holding my trembling body. It's Derek; I can tell by his scent; his mint body wash and his earthy cologne. I grip his arm and hold on for a few minutes to ground myself. This happens every couple of weeks and Derek is always there to wake me. He stays with me until my pulse settles, then gets up and leaves without looking at me or speaking. This shit is getting old and he needs to get over the fact I overstepped his boundary. If you share a house and fuck on the sofa, it's an open invitation as far as I see it. He clearly was having issues with me sticking around for the show.

I look at the clock. 4 a.m.; there's no way I'm going back to sleep tonight. I kick off the covers and head for the shower.

* * * * *

I'm not looking forward to introducing Hannah to River, my nerves are all over the fucking place. I know she's not going to like her and that just makes this whole shit worse. Sammy had been trying to get me to settle down, find a chick to comfort my dick on the regular.

"*You need to think about the future, Jasp,*" he droned on. But we nearly didn't get a future, so I want to live every day like it's my last.

Hannah stopped that shit when she turned up with a stick that had *pregnant* written on a tiny screen. I won't lie; I'm man enough to admit I nearly passed the fuck out. I had been putting it to Hannah for a few weeks. I didn't usually stick around for another go unless the chick was filthy, and despite the fact Hannah came from money and could be prudish in front of people, she was a fucking wild lay. So I stuck around for a while and now I'm paying for it.

River is the only female I've ever cared about. When I first met her, I wanted to be balls deep inside her, I won't lie, and any hot-blooded male would. She's insanely hot; bite down on your fist, and squeeze your eyes shut because you think you'll come in your pants if you don't hot! But she was with a fucking possessive predator that was insane and had been abusing her for years. She was also the love of my best friend, Sammy's, life. He was crazy for that girl. The good kind of crazy, and she was crazy in love with him too, so she became family to me.

Due to the aftermath of her then boyfriend, we had a bond between us that's unbreakable; pure and true. I fucking love those two and their little person, Michael. They are my family.

I had lost my mom—well, I can't say lost; you can't lose what you never really had. I don't even remember her; she died when I was a baby. I was raised by my dad. He was a good father, but I learned from his years of heartache over losing my mom that I don't want to love or be loved by a woman. The pain of losing them was a cross too heavy to bear.

Now I do love a woman; River. She pushed her way in, though not in a romantic way. I love her like family and would die for her, and nearly did. She's the strongest person I know; she's been through more than any person should ever go through. I watched a guy hit on her once. He asked if it hurt when she fell from heaven. She scoffed at him and replied, "I came from the pits of hell and I fucking clawed my way out. I didn't fall from nowhere."

No truer words spoken. She does have cracks and scars to live with, but so do Sammy and I. So we fill the cracks of each other and let the parts that won't heal stay broken. You can't claw your way out of hell and not have the scorch marks to prove it. My scorch marks haunt me in dreams.

I'm really not looking forward to leaving Derek's to move in with Hannah, but I can't very well ask Derek if she can stay here. He still isn't talking to me after I walked in on him with some posh chick straddling his lap. I took a seat, took my dick in hand, and enjoyed the free show. He was staring at my dick with… I don't know whether he was jealous of my size or what, but when our eyes locked and we came, I have never felt a connection like it, and never felt any kind of sexual connection with a male before him. It freaked me the hell out, and clearly him too as he hasn't looked me in the eye since. I tried to rationalise it to myself as him just staring at my size. I get it. My joy rider is pretty impressive; he could intimidate the Hulk.

But the voice in the back of my mind keeps telling me different things. If it was just him being weirded out by two men coming together, then I can't change that it happened. I haven't come that hard before ever; that's something I don't want to address either. I just hope he'll drop it and move on soon.

I never did see that woman again; maybe she wasn't so open to my voyeurism, judging by her screech and arm waving I think that could've been it. I don't get it. I fucking love all types of sex and I'm open to new things; threesome, foursome, orgy, kinky or vanilla, dirty or clean, slow or hard. As long as I come, I'm open to give it all a go.

I toot the horn and wait for Hannah to come out of the dance Studio River owns. I met her in a deli when I stopped to pick up sandwiches for Sammy and me one afternoon. We both reached for a bottle of water and both let go when we realized the other had hold of it. It fell right on my foot. She was really apologetic and bought my sandwich, so I bought her dinner. She was flirty and seemed up for only having a good time until she turned up with her pregnancy test, then out came her real personality. She was controlling and self-involved and moody. One innocent stop for a sandwich. Now look where I am. Hannah had decided to take her little sister along today when I told her River owned it. Coming to the dance studio is like slow torture for one reason. Kyra. She's a dance instructor here...

She stirs something inside me, primal and deep, that I refuse to give knowledge to. She's also my wet fucking dream. I want inside that tight little body so bad, but she's important to River, and as bad as I want her, I know I won't want her for longer than my needs take to be satisfied. So I don't pursue her, even though when she smiles at me, all nervous and coy, my dick strains against my jeans. I have to hold him there to stop him from tearing through and slithering up her leg. Now look at me, fucking locked into a relationship I don't want to be in with a kid on the way I had never planned on having.

My thoughts vanish when the door to the studio opens and Kyra steps out with *fucking* Hannah and her sister in tow. Kyra's eyes find mine and she offers a timid wave. She looks so sweet in her skin tight leggings and tank top. Fuck, her body is lean, but she still has curves in all the right places. Her dark red hair looks like the colour of the fancy wine Derek drinks; her pouty red lips would look so perfect around my dick. It twitches to life with my thoughts, but it's her eyes that do it for me. They're dark green like the grass in winter, and they have a sparkle like small pieces of crystal embedded in an emerald.

Fuck! What a pussy I'm being. Crystal in emeralds? What the fuck?

I tilt my head to get a good angle of her ass; that's the Jasper I'm comfortable with. I watch Hannah say bye to her sister; she's sending her home in a car with a driver, no one else. I jump from the car and walk over. Kyra folds her arms over her chest and looks down at the floor.

"What the fuck, Hannah? You can't send her home on her own with just a driver."

"Do you have to say the 'F' word?" She glares at me.

Is this chick for real? I've been saying the "F" word the whole eight weeks we've been together and I've been doing the "F" word to her. I see Kyra's body gently shaking and I know she's laughing.

"Something tickling you, Ky?" I inwardly groan at my own choice of words. I have something to tickle her with.

"Not yet, but things are looking up." She smiles and waves to someone pulling up behind us. No fucking way! Derek pulls up, and Kyra strokes Hannah's sister on the head before taking off into Derek's car. That shifty motherfucker! What the fuck is he doing with Kyra?

Derek

Jasper's nightmares, and the frantic call from River telling me Michael pushed her down the stairs, her sobbing cries telling me he was Danny's, left me really not feeling up for company tonight.

Danny still haunts us after six long years. I would never change the family I ended up with from the rubble of Danny's earth-shattering actions, but I'm so angry that they're still suffering, and would give anything to take away the damage he inflicted.

People don't realise trauma stays with you. It may fade, it may become easier to cope with, but it's like scar tissue; it'll always be there and no amount of healing can rid you of it.

Not all scars are visible. Sometimes the worst are the ones you can't see; they're the ones that hold your mind hostage in nightmares. They're the ones that manipulate your emotions, making guilt crawl into your mind, polluting reasonable thought. Guilt can be so hard to live with; consuming and painful.

People think death is the worst thing that can happen, but it's not, it's the living that other people have to go on doing once someone we love is taken from this world. It's the *what ifs* that constantly replay in our minds. It's the *did they know I loved them*? What would they be like if they were here now? How do I get up today and live with this agony?

The only thing that makes it slightly easier is having family to live for, to love, to get up and go on coping for. River has become like a sister to me. She fills a void left by my own sister; her death still plagues me and I feel responsible for her taking her life. River and I share this same grief. We're bonded by a shared misery; a painful sorrow that is a part of us.

Sammy has become like the brother I never had. We share a love for River, but also we are survivors. We've both looked the devil in the eye and lived to breathe another day.

Jasper; he's a different story. I struggle with how I feel about him. At first, he was just part of the River/Sammy package, and his constant string of easy whorish women grated on my nerves. But over time, I noticed subtle changes in him; the way he adores River and listens intently whenever she speaks; not like a boy with a crush, but like a child worshipping an enigma. He's fiercely loyal to Sammy, a trait I respect. He's loving, caring, funny, and so handsome I want to tear his clothes off, but although I'm comfortable with my bisexual sexuality, I don't think any of them know I like both men and women. I'm not sure if it would affect the relationship we have. Although I'm not ashamed of who I am, I can't risk losing them if they do have a problem with it. What would Jasper think if he knew I want more than friendship from him?

*****

I pull up at Twinkle Toes, River's dance studio. I'm here to pick up Kyra, a dance instructor at the studio. I know Jasper is interested in her, and rightly so, she is pure beauty. She's timid and has an air of innocence about her. I wouldn't usually date a victim of an ongoing investigation, her stalker one or any other, but Kyra is a friend of River's. I've run into her a few times because of her association with River and I tried to stay clear of her before this.

I remember the first time I saw her. I thought straight away that Jasper would be in her pants by the end of the first week. She's stunning; deep red locks of hair falling over her petite shoulders, but when her demure eyes met mine, they told me she was innocent. Too innocent for the likes of Jasper or me.

"This is Derek, the guy I was telling you about!" River said.

I narrowed my eyes at her. I've heard that sentence roll off her tongue a few times in the last few years, and not once had I taken her up on the numerous dates she had tried to send me on.

I wasn't looking for a girlfriend. I wasn't sure I could offer anyone what they would clearly need from a guy and unlike Jasper, I wouldn't just take one of River's set up dates to my bed, then ditch her. River had chased Jasper around my house for an hour straight when he took one of her dance instructors to bed and then made her take the walk of shame. She couldn't face River, so she quit her job. River lectured him on respect for her and the women he meets through her, finishing up with how his manhood would turn green and fall off if he wasn't careful.

I had managed to avoid most contact and date set ups with Kyra until fate decided to push us together when Twinkle Toes flagged up on the system. I remember that day two weeks ago as if it was yesterday.

"Hey, Jefferson. Your girl's studio came up when we ran

a check on this new stalker complaint." A uniformed officer named Greer said, approaching me at the coffee pot. I followed his eyes across the precinct and they collided with the green emeralds of Kyra's. She was chewing on her bottom lip and swirling a strand of her red locks around her index finger. Her foot tapped against the tile floor; she looked nervous and unbelievably pure and stunning. Every dominant man fibre inside me awoke and wanted to march over to her, throw her over my shoulder, and hide with her in a cave just so no other man could be graced with the vision of her beauty.

When realisation of what he said sank in, I had an almost possessive need to protect her and keep her with me so she could never face harm, and that feeling unsettled me. My head space was a mess already with the increasing lust I had for Jasper driving me insane without Kyra adding to my messed up thoughts, but it was too late. Some sick pervert was preying on young women; two had been beaten and one sexually assaulted in their homes after filing stalker claims. This was unacceptable. We had nothing on this guy, no DNA left at the scene or on the victims. No description, just notes he left them, all along the same lines:

I'm watching you.
I will strike and no one can save you.
You are my message.

His victims are in their early twenties, which is all we have to connect them. No other pattern, which leaves us with nothing to chase, no one to investigate. Kyra is convinced her note is from an ex-boyfriend who we haven't located yet, but it fits the case and I won't take the risk. So I decided Kyra was going to be glued to me until we find who's sending her the notes.

    Being around her has only intensified the need to keep her with me always and safe from harm. River doesn't need any more darkness in her life. She loves deep and cares for her friends. She gave her friendship to Kyra, therefore I will too. That's why I'm doing this. I tell myself that same thing every day.

* * * * *

    Kyra lives in a shitty part of town and doesn't drive, that's why I'm here tonight picking her up to take her home to change before our family dinner night back at mine.

    She's already outside the studio when I pull into a parking spot. She's standing next to some woman in a cashmere sweater and pencil skirt; the woman's hair is pulled back so tight it lifts her eyebrows and she seems to be having a debate with… *oh great, that's Jasper.*

    I leave the car running, so Kyra knows I'm not getting out. I still can't look at Jasper without picturing him sitting on the arm chair opposite me, rubbing his impressive cock while Caroline, the secretary of my lawyer's office, rode me. She had been flaunting her ass at me for months before I was drunk enough to eventually take her home one night after bumping into her at a bar. She was as boring as I knew she would be. I struggled to keep hard until Jasper walked up behind her, took his cock in hand and took a seat. I shivered when he stroked himself. He was so smooth and effortless, gliding his closed fist up and down his shaft. I had fantasied about being with him in sexual situations so often that I wasn't sure if I was imagining him sitting there or not. Caroline bounced in a mundane rhythm, no hip twists, just up and down while moaning.

"Ohhhh."

God, she was stale, but Jasper's grip and firm thrusts into his fist had my body on fire. I know he doesn't realise I want him, but he sure looked like he was putting on a show all for me.

Living with him over the last five years has been bittersweet; bitter because I want to pin him against the wall and fuck him till he roars my name, but he has no idea I play both sides and I know he definitely doesn't. I've only ever seen him with cheap sluts and as hard as it is to deny myself the release I crave from him, I wouldn't want to not have him in my life. So that's where the sweet comes in. We're close friends and I know he doesn't understand why I'm acting off with him. It's not for the reasons he thinks it is, it's because he makes it hard, literally, and I can't look at him at the moment without seeing him in the height of coming.

"Hey, thanks for doing this. I could have gotten the bus," Kyra says with a shy smile. Slipping into the passenger seat, I was too busy recalling Jasper that night to notice the door open. She's gorgeous, bewitching. "It's no problem." I lift the corner of my mouth in a brief smile before backing out. Kyra looks at Jasper with longing in her gaze. Join the club, beautiful Kyra.

Jasper

I groan as I pull up at the mansion with Hannah and Hannah's little sister. I'm not looking forward to this. She rubs her hand down her skirt and smiles over at me sweetly. I try not to scrunch my nose up at her. Damn, I'm so sick of her already; I don't know how I'm going to cope living with her. I know one thing; there's no way in hell she'll be the only one getting my dick. I'm already dreading ever letting her near it again.

I open the car door and slip out, opening the back for the kid. I wait for Hannah to round the car and she slips her hand in mine. This is such fucking bullshit. River will go off it when I tell her Hannah's carrying my kid. She'll see straight through me. She'll know I don't want to be with her.

The front door bursts open and River's infectious smile beams at me. "Hey, baby. Come," she says while wiggling her fingers, signaling me to get in her arms. I had been avoiding her, so she didn't corner me and pump me for information. She can read me like no other and she would have made her mind up about Hannah before ever meeting her. Hannah stiffens beside me when River calls me baby, but River calls all three of us baby. She kept doing it by accident to begin with. She was so used to saying it to Sammy, it just slipped out all the time because we all lived together, so over time, she just decided to call us all baby, and even after she moved out it stuck. We all fucking like it. It makes us feel wanted and loved, and we are. River is the only female in our group and she takes her role of looking after us very seriously.

I drop Hannah's hand to embrace River. She vibrates with excitement and I almost feel guilty that she isn't getting a fellow female she can love and do shit with. I release my hold when she does and drop a kiss to her cheek.

"I brought a playmate for Mikey. Where's my boy?"

River pales. I reach up and stroke her cheek. "Hey, what's wrong?"

She quickly recovers and shakes her head. "Nothing I just, erm, you have to keep an eye on them while I dish up," she murmurs.

I furrow my brow. "Okay."

I smile and she grips my arm. "I mean it, don't leave them alone together."

I can't help the chuckle that escapes my throat. "He's five River. He won't even care if she's a girl." Confusion shadows her face, then clears with a subtle shake of head.

"Come bring your woman through. I thought she was an illusion," Sammy shouts from the kitchen.

Mikey comes barreling around the corner and collides with my legs, wrapping his small frame around me.

"Hey, buddy." I reach down to pick him up, his smile just like his momma's. "I have a present for you in my room. Go find it," I challenge, putting him back to his feet.

Michael is the only reason I think I might be an okay dad. I fucking love that kid and would do anything for him. He's the bright light from a very dark time.

I reach back for Hannah's hand and drag her through to the kitchen. Sammy's eyebrows nearly disappear into his hairline when he catches a glimpse of her. She looks like a legal secretary in what she's wearing—not dinner attire at all.

Sammy stands next to me as I release Hannah's hand and turns to face her. "Hannah, this is Sammy."

Her eyes take on a dreamy look, glossing over, and a smirk tilts her perfect lips.

I can't help the grin I give her. Yeah, Sammy is a good-looking guy. Together in college we had chicks begging us to take them home. A lot of people thought we were brothers. We both have dark hair and blue eyes; however, Sammy is bigger built than me. I keep a tight, trim physique.

Her eyes trail between the two of us. She is fucking high if she thinks she stands a chance at getting a go with Sammy. Did she not see River? Hannah isn't bad looking, but she isn't River; River is a grade A beauty.

"Look what Uncle Jasp bought me!" Mikey's voice carries through the kitchen. He's holding up the game console I bought him.

Sammy's hand clips me around the head. "You spoil him."

I shrug, "That's my job."

River stares at Mikey, her eyes stormy like when she's struggling with all her emotions. I wave my hand in front of her face to distract her, and stand next to her in the kitchen. "You okay, River?"

Her lips turn up into a weak smile. "Yeah I was just thinking about when I was pregnant with him."

I smile back at her. I remember her feet swelling and me having to help her with her socks. Her eyes lock onto Hannah, who looks uncomfortable at the other side of the room.

"She's not right for you."

I close my eyes. I knew she would pick up on my fake feelings.

"You deserve to be loved and to fall in love, Jasp. It's the most amazing feeling in the world. I want that for you," she whispers.

"She's pregnant, River."

I watch the wonder, then disappointment cloud her beautiful eyes. Fuck, it hurt to see that in her eyes, to know I put it there.

"How did this happen?" I raise an eyebrow and she points her finger at me. "I know how you make a child, Jasp. I mean, you've always been adamant you're careful." She looks at Hannah again and runs her hand through her hair. She's pissed.

"I am careful. I have no idea how this happened, River."

She closes the few steps separating our bodies and wraps her tiny arms around my shoulders, bringing my head down into the crook of her neck. I bind a firm grip around her waist and breathe in her comfort; she smells like home and she is my home. I feel so fucking lost at sea at the moment. I squeeze her extra tight to gain as much comfort as possible.

"You'll be an amazing father, Jasp. I just wanted you to have this with someone you love." Her soft lips press against my temple.

"Hey, stop stealing my wife, you have your own woman now." Sammy grins. "She's not what I expected I must admit." He laughs.

The sound of the front door opening saves me from speaking. Sounds of movement fill the lobby as River goes off to greet the guests.

"Kyra!" River beams as she's met at the kitchen entrance by her friend. "I'm so glad you could make it." She wraps her in an embrace.

Derek stands behind her, his eyes finding mine for the first time since the night we came together. There's something in his eyes I can't decipher, and he has me squirming like a teenage girl. He has such a commanding presence. His eyes scan the room, resting on Hannah and a look of distaste falls over his features.

"Let's eat," Sammy bellows to River who is whispering something to Derek. He rubs down her arms and looks to be comforting her. She nods her head and grips onto him. He pulls her close, his strong arms wrapping her in a safe cocoon. I know the comfort and safety that embrace offers. It's the same one that rescues me from my nightmares.

Kyra's green eyes smile as she passes me, her red hair flowing like a veil down her back. She's changed into tight as fuck jeans that squeeze her ass as she walks. Her green silk top makes her eyes stand out even more than they already did.

"Now, that's more like it," Sammy croons into my ear. I hadn't even realised he had approached me; my eyes were glued to the red-haired beauty sauntering towards the dining room.

Derek

River was trembling when I held her. She told me she wanted Michael and Sammy to have DNA tests done. I told her that after I drop Kyra off tonight, I'll stop by hers, so we can talk. I need to get inside her head and try to reason with her irrational thoughts.

"Who wants wine?" Sammy asks once we're all seated at the table. Jasper's woman and Kyra hold out their glasses. Sammy fills them, then brings beer for us and water for River. I look at her questioningly. River developed a taste for wine from me, so to see her drinking water has me raising a brow.

"I'm pregnant!" She beams at me, then her smile falters and her eyes go to Michael who's staring back at her.

"There must be something in the water." An annoying high-pitched voice speaks over the silence that's fallen over the table. I want to congratulate River and Sammy, but the odd statement coming from Jasper's date has me staring at her. Jasper glares at her and Sammy chokes on the beer he's in the middle of chugging.

"What the fuck?" Sammy questions.

"Hannah's pregnant," Jasper groans.

"Is it yours?" Sammy fires back. I feel Kyra shift in her seat.

"Excuse me?" Hannah whines.

Sammy's eyes are trained on Jasper. "Jasper, what the fuck, man?" He stands and rubs his hands down his face "I know, Sammy. I don't know how the fuck this happened, but it did and now I have to do what's right by Hannah and my kid."

I feel sick; Jasper will stay with this girl to do the right thing. He's going to be a father. Shit! I didn't see this coming.

"I've lost my appetite. Come, Rebecca," Hannah says, snapping her fingers at a young girl sat next to Michael. The little girl rises to her feet and follows Hannah.

"Hannah, wait that was rude of him. Please stay, this is just really surprising is all. We're sorry for the outburst," River calls after Hannah's retreating form.

"I know this is a big shock, but it was for me too and I need your support," Jasper says before he follows Hannah out of the house.

I need some hard liquor; this beer isn't going to do anything for me. I stand and go over to my bar with Sammy hot on my heels.

"Did you know about this? Is this why you and he aren't talking?"

I spin to face him.

"No, I had no idea, but it kind of makes sense why he kept this one around." I ignore his observation of me and Jasper not speaking. Sammy sits on a stool and chin lifts to a bottle of Jim Beam.

"I can't believe he knocked someone up. He was always so fucking adamant he would never make that kind of mistake." I pour him four digits worth and watch as he downs it one go and gestures for me to refill.

"Accidents happen. He'll be a great father," I reply as the deep, dark hole inside me grows bigger by the second.

"I don't doubt he'll be a great father, but to stay with a woman he clearly doesn't love, maybe doesn't even like, is stupid for whatever reason."

Kyra

I breathe in the aromas surrounding the table; the pot roast sitting in the centre mocks me. I was ravenous when I got here and haven't had a real home cooked meal since I left home four years ago.

I leisurely inch my spoon closer to the pot when my body becomes motionless. The beat of my heart slows each thump pulsing heavy in my chest as the announcements begin. I should have known there was a reason Jasper was with Hannah; River told me Jasper liked to play the field, so no matter how much my body vibrates with hidden need when it is around him, I know it's a feeling I'll never give relief to.

I can't be one in a long run of many; I value myself and my body more than that. My body is a gift for a partner who loves me, so Jasper will just have to remain a fantasy.

I cared about him ever since he first walked in and began dancing with River; his adoration for her is endearing and sparks an emotion right in my core just for him. I know he finds me attractive; Jasper's eyes are very expressive, and he isn't shy when blatantly checking out my body. He's beautiful. His dark hair makes the light blue of his eyes sparkle. He has full lips that lift into the most devilish smirk whenever he's teasing or staring at me.

I knew getting close to Derek was a bad idea with him living and being so close to Jasper. It'll force me to be around Jasper a lot more than before, but Derek has such a strong powerful presence. I feel as though I need to be near him; he makes me feel safe, content, wanted for more than just my body. When he looks at me, he really looks at *me* as a person, and that's why I'm sitting here, smelling a dinner I more than likely won't be able to stomach anymore.

"Kyra, help yourself." I look over to River. She, Michael, and I are the only ones left at the table. I hear Derek and Sammy having a discussion in the other room, but strain to hear what's being said.

"I want you to be manager at the studio. I'll need to take it easy and attend doctor appointments and maternity leave."

I'm sure my jaw is on the table. I've only been at the studio eight months and in those eight months, River and I have become close, but there are other dancers there that have more experience than me yet she wants me. I feel honored and proud of myself. I moved away to make a life and this is a huge opportunity.

"Think it over and get back to me."

I raise my wine to my lips and gulp down the whole contents. "I accept, thank you."

"Good." She smiles back at me. Her eyes dart to Michael who's looking back at her. Maybe she's worried about him seeing the little episode with Jasper and Hannah. I reach for the pot of food in front of me and help myself to a portion, so I don't seem rude. Derek reappears and takes his seat next to me.

"Dinner smells good, Riv. I'll talk to Jasper." Her gentle nod ends the conversation as everyone begins to eat.

Sammy doesn't come back to the table and the

atmosphere leaves me wanting to go home and crawl into my bed, and pretend Jasper's news didn't happen.

Derek

I drive Kyra home and kiss her gently on the cheek before leaving her safely locked inside her apartment. My mind is on Jasper and his news. I'm not sure if he'll be home when I get there. River and Sammy left just before me, so I'm hoping to get to sit down with him.

The incoming call from the station was the last thing I needed. "Jefferson."

"Hey, it's Masters. We have an incident and the victim asked us to call you. A Lake. Caroline Lake?"

Shit!

"What happened?"

"She was attacked getting into her car. There was note on her windscreen and we think this is connected to the stalker case."

"Where did it happen?"

"At her office."

Shit, what was she doing there at this time on a Saturday? That woman needs to take a fucking break. She's a workaholic.

"I'm on my way."

Fifteen minutes later, I pull up at my lawyer's office. An ambulance and two squad cars are parked up, their red and blue lights lightening the darkened sky.

"Jefferson." A uniform nods his head at me. I go straight to the ambulance and wince when Caroline's bruised face comes into view. Her eye is swollen shut and her cheek's a deep red-purple colour. Her blouse is ripped open showing her white lace bra.

"Cover her up," I growl, angry that they haven't already.

"Derek?" she sniffles.

"It's okay, can you tell me what happened?"

"He came from nowhere. I was just getting to my car and I noticed a note."

A whimper leaves her. "Someone grabbed my hair and forced my head into the bonnet. My legs gave out and I couldn't see very well, but he grabbed at my blouse to hold me up while he punched me." An uncontrolled sob shakes her entire body. I jump into the ambulance and pull her into me.

"It's okay, ssshhh."

* * * * *

"They want to keep her overnight. I want you to get her statement while it's fresh in her mind. Have forensics run that note for fingerprints," I tell Hance while I rub the crease I know is furrowing my brow.

I hate men who do this kind of violence to women, and we have nothing to go on, so this is going to keep happening.

I slip into my car and check the time. Four hours it's been since I got that call; this day has turned out to be a nightmare. I drive the six miles home, the rain washing the day away as it batters against the car.

Jasper

Thud, Thud, Thud. Every time my foot hits the treadmill, the impact echoes around the room. The sweat has soaked down my bare torso and runs into the waistband of my sweatpants. With every thud, the memory of Danny's gun going off flashes into my thoughts. I try to think about what happened earlier and the drive back with Hannah. Listening to her talking drove me in-fucking-sane. It's true men fade women out when they go on a verbal rampage; twenty minutes we had been in the car and she was still going on.

"Jasper, seriously?" she whined.

Her heavy sigh forced me roll my eyes. Shit! Am I really going to take the plunge with this chick? Can I live day in and day out coming home to her?

"Your friends were rude, implying the baby isn't yours."

I pulled up on her drive and inwardly groaned when I saw her dad's Mercedes parked on the drive. The front door opened and out stepped her mother dressed in a pencil skirt, blouse, and suit jacket, hair neatly pinned back, nothing out of place as she air kissed Hannah's cheeks and gestured for the kid to go inside. "We have a wedding to plan. We need to make an appointment to have you fitted for your dress before you start showing." She looked down at Hannah's almost flat stomach and sneered. "Anymore then you already are."

I couldn't be around them. I drove around trying to clear my thoughts and then decided to work myself into exhaustion on the treadmill. My mind can't focus on distracting myself with other thoughts, Danny and the left over anxiety are willful tonight. I push harder, but nothing helps me escape the images. My feet come down harder.

Thud, thud, thud. The sound, and then instant pain rips through my flesh, the warmth of my life flowing from me at an uncontrolled rate; the dizziness makes my head swim. River's voice, her scream a distant echo as the darkness closes in around me, suffocating me in the fear that I may never open my eyes again.

Swiping at the sweat trickling into my face, I notice it's red in colour–*blood*.

"What the fuck?"

I look down my body. It's also red; I'm bleeding. I'm covered in blood. What's happening? Fear grips me in a vice hold.

"Wake up, you're dreaming. It's just a dream, Jasp. Wake up!"

Derek, Derek? That's Derek. I'm dreaming. I gasp for breath; I grasp on to him, the sweat clinging to my skin, leaving a musky scent in the air.

Two nightmares. Two nights in a row.

Fuck!

Derek moves from the bed, but I jump up to stop him. "Don't, don't go yet, please." I know I sound weak, but I need him here right now. His eyes are trained on my naked form. I sleep naked and when I jumped up to stop him, the sheet had fallen away.

"Der, why you staring at my junk? You've seen it before,

man," I joke, trying to lighten the tense atmosphere, but it has the opposite effect.

Holy shit! Is he blushing?

"Der?" I ask, confused. I've never seen Derek flustered, but he looks embarrassed. What the fuck?

"You should see the therapist again for these nightmares," he tells me as he marches from my room, leaving me completely bewildered.

* * * * *

The light bleeds through the blinds, casting a warm glow over the room. I couldn't get back to sleep after the weird shit with Derek last night, so I just laid here and tried to make sense of everything. It didn't work.

I drag the covers off and head for the shower. I prepare myself to have to deal with Sammy and River today. Hannah emailed me last night—not picked the phone up. She fucking emailed me, stating we need to gradually get used to her idea of being a bigger part of each other's lives and start the move in process. Apparently that starts with her letting me do the shopping. What kind of test is that? I don't shop, so when she's eating Cheetos and cereal for dinner later she better not complain.

I wash the dry sweat from my nightmare off my body in the shower. I slip into a clean shirt and jeans, and run my hands through my messy hair before going downstairs for coffee. The smell in the air is one more thing I'll miss when I move out. Derek always makes a fresh pot of coffee every morning without fail.

I follow the tempting aroma into the huge kitchen. This place is too big for two guys to live in; this kitchen could keep a hotel in food service alone. Derek stands with a mug in hands, his suit neatly pressed with nothing out of place. I can see why Kyra is attracted to him. Derek is a good-looking man; he has that whole dark mysterious shit going on for him, and he also has an air of confidence that makes even guys take notice.

"Hey," I say with a head nod.

"Hey," he responds, still not looking at me.

"Listen, Der, I know I overstepped with that chick, but this is getting old now." I walk right up to him, our bodies a breath away. He lifts his head, so he's looking me in the eye. "I need my friend right now. I promise not to do that shit again. I'll even apologise to the chick if you want to bring her back here."

He squints his eyes and seems to be studying me; I shift under his scrutiny. He steps forward, his chest touching mine, his warm breath whispering across my cheeks. "I'll always be your friend."

I have never felt anything like this; I'm a man who's banged his way through many a woman. I've been in the presence of some good-looking men, and men of power, but no one, not a women nor a man has ever made me feel the way I'm feeling, and I'm not even sure what the fuck this is I am feeling. Derek is too close, his eyes too emotional, too personal. His body is having an effect on mine, a sexual effect. I step back and shake my head.

What the fuck, Jasp? I risk a glance up at Derek; he has a raised eyebrow like he knows what I'm thinking. My head spins as I feel a knot twist my stomach.

"Cool," I say before I scurry from the kitchen without my coffee. I need to be away from him. I'm losing my fucking mind. I need to get out of here.

I head for the coat closet and find the console I bought

Michael in there, smashed up. "What the hell?"

"What?" I jump at the sound of Derek behind me, the sneaky fuck. I didn't realise he had followed me out.

I grab up the console and lift it for him to see. "I got this for Michael." Derek's brow furrows in thought. "What's going on?"

He exhales hard. "Has River not said anything to you about Michael?"

I immediately go taut and alert. "No, what? What's wrong with Michael?"

Derek notices my stiff posture, rests a hand on my shoulder and rubs. Such an innocent gesture that he's done many times before, so why is my stomach bottoming out and why is it leaving a fire trail in its wake?

"He's fine. She's convinced herself he's Danny's. She said he pushed her down the stairs."

That shakes me from my Derek-confused state. "What? I need to see her. Is she still seeing her therapist? She needs to get over this shit," I grumble, gaining me a smirk from Derek.

"She needs to get over her shit, yet you still have night terrors?"

I glare back at him. "I don't think my kid's trying to fucking kill me." I'm being a defensive prick, but I need this emotion. It's better than what I was feeling seconds ago.

His deep laugh echoes in the lobby. "Give it time, yours isn't here yet."

That empty feeling creeps over me. Hannah! God, how could I let this happen? I slip my jacket on and leave without saying goodbye.

* * * * *

Shopping is not my thing. I hate the supermarkets from the parking to the harmless looking fragile old ladies who would wrestle you to get the next bargain. Their innocent *"Yes, dear," "No, dear," "Can you reach and pass me this, dear?"* to trolley ramming you and queue jumping. *Fragile my ass*!

I manage to fill a trolley and get it to the register and out the store without cursing every ancient lady who abuses her old age position.

Hannah's apartment is spotless. It's hard to believe anyone actually lives here; the white walls in every room give it a sterile feel; it's cold and lifeless—like its owner. I hate shopping, but putting the groceries away is even worse. I don't know where she keeps everything, so if she complains, it'll be her doing all grocery shops in the future. *Fuck*, that made me shudder… a future with Hannah.

I set up my laptop and get to work sorting the accounts for the new business. Sammy and I are opening a new garage in the next town over. Hannah hates the trade I'm in. She thinks I should be doing more with my business degree, but I'm happy doing this. I have money from my mom's life insurance that I've never needed to touch. Hannah doesn't know about it and I earn a good income being in business with Sammy.

The front door opening and closing draws my attention to Hannah huffing towards me. "I got off early. My parents dropped the bomb that they'll be dining with us tonight so I wanted to make sure you got decent groceries."

She opens the fridge, pulls out a half open bottle of wine, and pours herself a glass.

"You can't drink that!" I point to the glass while I walk towards her.

She rolls her eyes. "One is fine Jasper."

I reach for the glass before she can take a sip. "I'd prefer that you didn't. River never drank when she was pregnant."

Her mechanical laugh makes a cold chill race up my spine. "Well, I'm not your precious River, Jasper, so give me the glass." She holds her hand out to me. I walk in her direction, but bypass her to the sink and empty the contents of the glass down the drain. I can feel her glare in the back of my head, but I don't give a shit. I rinse the glass and leave it on the drainer. Her inhaling and exhaling sounds like a bull and I'm the red flag. I ignore her and walk back into the lounge. Her opening and slamming cupboard doors makes me smile. Day one; one fucking day and we are already failing.

"Jasper!" Her screech has me bolting into the kitchen.

"What, what happened?"

"What is this?"

I look to the offending item she's waving around at me. "It's flavored lube, pussy lick. It says it right there on the tube."

She stamps her foot like a six-year-old. "Why is it in my food cupboard?"

"What? I don't see the problem, you let me keep the ketchup in there." She shakes her head, clearly confused. I reach in the cupboard and pull out the ketchup. "Condiments. We put them on the things we like to eat. The ketchup… you keep it here in the cupboard. I put this on the things I like to eat." I put the ketchup back and grimace at the deep shade of red she turned. "What if my mother had found this, what would she think?"

I snatch the lube from her frantic waving hands. "My daughter picked good, lucky her?"

"You are such a dick. The fact that you're good with it is the only reason I keep you around." She glares at me.

"The fact that you're carrying my kid is the only reason

I'm here," I bite back.

She leers. "We don't have to be fond of each other, Jasper. We can work like a partnership if you just climb aboard, that's what a marriage is, a business transition."

I squint my eyes at her. "How fucking depressing is that, Hannah? Fuck this, I'm done playing house for today." I pack up my stuff and head for the front door.

"What about dinner?"

I shrug my shoulders. "You have to book that shit in with my secretary." I close the door behind me as I leave to the sound of Hannah calling me an asshole. I don't want love, not after watching dad suffer, but a loveless marriage is something I want even less.

I drive around to kill a few hours before I head to the studio to see River. I pull up and just watch through the window as her and Kyra teach a few younger girls leg lifts and twirler shit. They both have such grace in their movements; it's like watching birds in the sky, effortless movements, mesmerizing.

I exit the car and head inside. Mikey sitting on the bench at the end of the studio brings a smile to my face. "Hey buddy." He doesn't look up at me, so I sit next to him. "What's up?"

He shrugs his little shoulders and looks over at River.

"So I found your games machine." I watch his eyes cast down to his shoes. "Don't you want to talk to your Uncle Jasp?"

His head snaps sharply in my direction, making me flinch from the dark gaze he pins me with. "You're not my uncle. I don't have one."

I watch as he darts off towards River, leaving me with a hollow feeling in my chest. We're real close and hearing that, even though he's only five and kids say cruel things without thought, it still guts me.

"Hey, baby. Would you mind taking Kyra home for me? I told Derek I would, but I need to leave early. Mikey has soccer practice," River says, coming over to me. I nod my head, getting to my feet and encompassing her in a hug. She leaves me watching Kyra teaching a young teenage girl. Kyra's beautiful in her movement. She even rivals River.

* * * * *

"You want to eat?" I ask her. She shuffles in her seat, making me smile, her perfume leaving her sweet scent in the car.

"Sure," she murmurs.

I drive us to a little Italian place I found through Hannah. In her email, she insisted we now do a date night there once a week, so we can catch up and inform each other of the things happening in our lives, even though we'll be living in the same house. This really has just turned into a business deal with her and I get depressed every time I think about having to take the next step and move in. Her mom can't wait to get us down the aisle. I still haven't even told my dad.

I pull up and get out of the car, going round to help Kyra out. Her timid smile pulls on something deep in my gut; she's so fucking cute. I walk behind her, so I can shamelessly watch her ass as she saunters forward into the restaurant.

I glare at the waiter for staring at Kyra's ass and grinning like a fat guy at an all you can eat buffet; he shrugs and raises an eyebrow. I narrow my eyes at him, watching as red heats his cheeks and he flees to the other side of the restaurant.

A young brunette greets us and shows us to a table for

two. We order a pasta dish and a glass of wine for Kyra, and iced water for myself.

"Tell me about you," I say, resting my elbows on the table and leaning forward. The glint in her eyes and pink tinge to her cheeks make my inner playboy grin; I affect her and just that knowledge affects me.

"What do you want to know?" She clears her throat as her hand comes up to brush her hair from her face.

"Everything. Tell me everything. How long have you danced?"

Her eyes light up and she smiles. "Since I was four. Ballet, tap, jazz, salsa, all leading me to my passion, contemporary."

I raise my eyebrows. "Salsa?"

Her laugh echoes around the restaurant. All eyes fall on her, but she doesn't notice. "That's all you got, huh?" She tilts her head to the side and smiles; it's a sexy confident smile, a flirty one I'm not used to from her. Dance is where she lives; it's where her confidence and passion is. I want to see her in her element; I want to watch her exist in the moment, in the movement of her passion.

"I want to take you dancing. Tonight we'll go."

She grins and shakes her head as she giggles. "No way do you go dancing."

"Hey, don't mock me. River forced me to be her partner many a times. She likes to go out to a dance club every now and then and if Sammy can't take her, I have to as Derek took her once and stood like a bodyguard stopping approaching men instead of dancing with her." Her eyes sparkle again. "I can't imagine Derek dancing."

I cringe and pretend to shudder, pulling another giggle from her. The waiter places our dishes in front of us. "So does your family support you?"

She swallows the food she just put in her mouth and hovers her hand in front. "I have two parents who love me, so they support all my decisions."

I smile.

We finish up dinner, then I take her back to her place, so she can change. It's small and needs decorating, although I notice the new locks on the door and smile.

"Derek," her shy voice murmurs against my shoulder. She tilts her head to the locks when I angle my head down to look at her. She's so close; her tiny frame heating my side, her scent so intoxicating I need to leave before I... don't leave. I could easily lose myself in this girl.

"Jasp." She looks up at me through her thick lashes. Shit, those fucking emeralds are captivating. "I'm ready," she says, and steps around me. She's in a knee length summer dress, green to match her eyes. I need to not drink. Keeping my thoughts from the gutter will be hard enough, but if I add alcohol, I'll have to have her.

"Jasp, you coming?"

Oh, God. I swallow the groan wanting to rip from me and follow her out the apartment.

The club is busy, the rhythmic beat pulsing through the room, the heat from people gyrating leaving a heavy haze in the air. I can see her body already bouncing with excitement. She spins to face me, a glorious smile spreads across her cheeks as she reaches her hands out to me.

"Come dance with me," she says, all giddy. She's adorable.

I nod towards the dance floor and follow behind her. The music has sexual intent written in every word; the mix of instruments creates a lustful beat as I move my body against hers, but she's a fucking pro and twists and bends all around me, her tight body brushing, rubbing against mine, her ass pushing into my crotch, making me hard as stone and dying to seek the warmth of her pussy.

Everyone has spread out, creating a circle around us, watching in awe of this amazing red-haired siren letting the music take her. The music and movements own this woman's soul and she owns the movements; it's amazing to watch her flawless body. She's perfection. Her dress lifts with every movement, teasing us with more flesh and a glimpse of the black panties covering the place every man in here wants to be. It takes all the self-control I have not to drag her out of here, back to mine, hers, the fucking alley. Instead I let her dance all over me and around me for hours until the sweat clings to our skin and fatigue sets into my limbs.

I drop her at her apartment with a kiss on the head and a promise to take her out again. I should get a fucking medal or an ice pack for the blue balls I'll be dealing with later.

Derek

Something isn't sitting right with me with these cases. I traced Kyra's ex; he's busy drinking his life away and paying twenty dollar hookers in the next town over from where he lives, so I know it's not him who sent Kyra the note.

I nearly lost my mind last night when I couldn't reach her. She finally called me back when Jasper sauntered in with a huge fucking grin on his face. I don't know what he thought he would achieve by spending time with her. He wouldn't pursue her as a one night stand out of respect for River and the new boundaries she had set him, and he couldn't have anything other than that because of Hannah, and let's face it—he's Jasper. He only wants a good time or two then they're gone and he's onto the next. Hannah really knew how to snag the playboy with her pregnancy. No matter how much of a slut he is, he has a good soul and will do what's right by her.

"Hey, you want?" he asks gesturing to his coffee mug, coming into the dining area wearing only sweatpants that are hung real low on his hips. He's so toned, muscle on bone and not an ounce of fat. He's athletic perfection and I want to test his stamina. "Derek!"

I look up at him. He's now standing a few feet from me.

"Here, I think you need it. You're doing that daydreaming staring shit." He laughs, handing me his coffee and slipping into the empty chair next to me. I can smell his skin, fresh from the shower and visions of him in there fill my head. God, I've lived six years and managed to mainly suppress these emotions, only giving permission to them when I would mourn the loss of the feelings I could never share.

"This the stalker case?"

His question tugs me from my musing. "Yes, he attacked again and I knew her." I pull on the documents I have scattered into a pile in front of me and sip on the coffee he gave me.

"Shit! Who?"

"A woman from my lawyer's office."

I watch recognition flash in his eyes and a small smile tilts his mouth briefly before it's gone and worry replaces it. "Is she okay? Did he…?"

I shake my head and stand. "No, she's banged up a little, but nothing of a sexual nature."

Jasper stands with me and grasps my arm, causing my eyes to rest on where his hand holds onto me. "Why is there a file on Kyra?"

I raise my eyes to meet his. "She received a note. She believes it's her ex, but I'm not so sure."

His brows pinch together. "So you think it's the same guy? Do you have anything on him? When did she get a note? Did he attack her?"

I watch his chest rise and fall. He's working himself up. "Jasp, she's fine and will stay fine. I'm looking out for her, which leads me to point out next time you decide to take her dancing, contact me, so I don't go out of my mind with worry."

His eyes have glazed over and his breathing is uneven. He's looking at me with an intensity I've not witnessed from him before; his eyes drop and I follow them to notice I grabbed his hip when trying to calm him. This isn't a friend touch and I pull my hand away before I go back to gathering the evidence.

"I need to get to the station," I mumble, and hurry past him. I feel the burn on the back of my neck from his gaze.

* * * * *

The station is busy, alive with phones ringing and friendly banter between officers. I'm young for the position I hold, but I earned my place here. I'm a great detective and all my energy is going into finding this sick son of a bitch. I know first-hand how quickly these things escalate. The more he gets away with, the bolder he'll become and more aggressive attacks will increase.

"Hans, I want all reports on this stalker case on my desk in ten," I say as I pass his desk.

"That's my case," he mumbles through a half-eaten pastry, brushing the crumbs off his shirt.

"Bring me the files," I command in my no argument tone. I watch him swallow and nod before I make my way to my office, foregoing the poor cup of coffee I usually pour when I get here.

I dial Kyra's number. It rings twice before she picks up. "Hey," she says down the line, making me stop my pacing of the office carpet.

"Hey," I reply and smile. "So you're up?"

"Yes, I just showered and now I'm waiting for River to come pick me up."

I exhale, nodding my head. "Okay, good. I want you to come over for food tonight. I'll pick you up after work." I hear her breathing and I swear I can feel her smile.

"Erm..."

I interrupt her before she can finish. "You're coming over to eat with me tonight, Kyra, and I'll pick you up after work." Her soft little breaths stir my desire.

"Okay."

I disconnect as the door opens and Hans places the files on my desk. "The latest letter is still in forensics."

I nod my head to the door, ordering him to leave without speaking. He nods in acknowledgement and leaves.

I open the first file and look over the incident reports. There's a pattern. I flick to the last page where the pictures are and stop breathing. I recognise her; she's my dry cleaning girl. She had been flirting and had given me her number a few weeks ago.

I grab the next file and flip to the back. A girl I stopped to help when her car had broken down. I took her for coffee.

Fuck!

The connection is me!

Someone is targeting women I know, or is this just coincidence?

I jump when my phone rings. Sammy's name flashes across the screen and I hit speaker. "What's up?" I ask, but there's a stutter in my speech.

"Hey, what's wrong?"

I roll my eyes. Sammy can pick up on all of our anxieties and it's fucking annoying. I'm sure River has been teaching him that women can tell a mile off when something is wrong, and Sammy is picking up her intuition.

"Nothing. Listen, this case, the stalker one, I haven't mentioned it to River because she has a lot going on, but this guy has sent a note to Kyra."

I hear a rustling and a door slam closed. "What the fuck? When?"

"A week and half ago."

I hear his panting, his anger building. "And you didn't think to mention anything sooner? Fuck, Derek! She spends most of her time with River!"

I stand and rub my hand over my head "I know. I've been on top of it, you know what River means to me, Sam. I would never let anyone hurt her or Kyra. I just want you to keep an extra eye on River just to be safe."

"I can't believe this shit. Who the fuck is this guy?"

"That's what I'm trying to figure out and until I do, I need to keep an extra eye out. Be vigilant."

"Oh, no one is coming near my fucking family. Never again, Derek, never a-fucking-gain. Keep this between us. River is vulnerable right now with Michael and the pregnancy, and she doesn't need any more stress."

"Vulnerable is never a word I'd use for River, but I agree. I don't want her to worry."

"I want you to do a DNA test through the station. I don't want her to know, but I need to know for sure just so I can either put her mind at rest or deal if Michael shares *his* DNA and not mine. Whatever happens, Michael is my son. He's my son, Derek, he's mine!"

I sit back down. "I know he is, Sam. I'll get it done, but I'll need a swab from both of you."

"I know, I'll get you them," he says before he hangs up.

I dial Hans' desk, telling him to get in my office.

Two minutes later he's filling my door frame. "What's up?"

"I want you to patrol Twinkle Toes. Keep your eye out for anything suspicious; any cars that seem to be loitering. I want everything, even if it's a tramp setting up camp, I want it checked and double checked." He nods his head and leaves.

I start compiling a list of any and all offenders I had a hand in putting away, then check to see if any have been released. If this is personal, they're definitely sending me a message.

Kyra

I feel it, the chill racing up my spine. The unsettling feeling of being watched has been with me since I woke. It isn't like when Jasper or Derek watches me; it's unnerving and leaves a sickly feeling in my stomach.

I hurry to River's SUV and slip in.

"Hey." She beams and passes me a latte. "So I want to go over the day to day running of Twinkle Toes today. Sammy is already demanding I cut back my hours there. He worries and has already been on the phone three times in the twenty minute drive here." She giggles; the love in her eyes when she talks of Sammy is an emotion I dream of having, and seeing in the eyes of someone when they talk about me. That heart-gripping emotion that obliterates every other feeling, thought, and sense. The sensation that leaves you gasping for breath and that infuses your soul, creating a moment in time so perfect, so overwhelming that it imprints itself in your memory for all other lovers and life changing moments to live up to. Love is something we all crave. It's in our DNA and lately I've found myself daydreaming about having it. The only problem is, my thoughts are conflicted about who I want it with.

"Why won't he bloody pass?" I pull myself from my thoughts as River hoots the horn, waving at a car to pass. The Mustang slowly pulls out and cruises past the SUV, its windows blacked out, so we can't see the driver.

"I bet he's totally flipping me off behind that glass," River states.

"What happened?"

She turns to look at me. "He was riding my ass and when I had to break, he broke hard, so I told him to go around."

I watch the car speed off. A shudder rocks my body, the sickly feeling still in the pit of my stomach.

We pull up at the studio. Sammy and Jasper are sitting in the car park, and River's eyebrows furrow as she switches off the ignition and slips out of the car. Sammy engulf her in his presence, his strong arms swallowing her in a tight hug. I slip out and smile at Jasper, my insides jumping as if I'd eaten a thousand grasshoppers. His pink tongue swipes over his bottom lip and I have to swallow the moan crawling up my throat.

"Hey." I nod and he smiles, leaning towards me to whisper in my ear.

"You owe me a massage."

I pull back and have to bite my lip. "And why is that?"

He rolls his shoulders. "Because last night you made me sweat more than I ever have."

I jerk back when a slap lands on Jasper's head. Sammy glares at him and River's mouth has popped open forming an "O" shape.

"Hey, you will slap one time too many one of these days," Jasper complains, rubbing the spot Sammy hit.

Sammy pushes his finger into Jasper's chest. "You better not have let the beast loose on Kyra. I swear, Jasp, I'll kick your ass."

Jasper scrunches his nose and squints his eyes. "I can do more than just fuck a woman, Sammy."

My eyes widen and the blush creep over my skin. "We went dancing, nothing more," I manage to squeak out.

Jasper's phone ringing breaks the uncomfortable moment. He swipes the screen and brings it to his ear while still glaring at Sammy. "Hey, what's up? I was busy last night. Well, you should have called. Are you okay? No, stay in bed. I'll go to the pharmacy and be there in half hour."

He ends the call and turns to Sammy. "Hannah has a bug, and I need to go make sure she's okay."

Sammy rolls his eyes and waves him off.

Sammy stayed all day despite me telling him he could kidnap his wife for the day. River kept shifting her eyes to him, curious as to why he was adamant to not leave. I tried to ignore the unsettling feeling plaguing me since this morning. Jasper hadn't returned and my mind couldn't seem to focus on anything but where he was, who he was with, and how stupid I was for letting him in, letting him affect me in anyway.

We could never be anything other than friends and I was also having feelings towards his friend. This could not be happening. I needed to stop thinking about him, and concentrate on work.

Derek

Her laughter fills the studio and caresses the walls, bouncing back towards me. It's been a long time, if ever, that a woman has bewitched me like Kyra seems to have. My mind is racing with possibilities for us; can I actually let her in? Can I love her?

As always, niggling in the darker corners are the thoughts, hopes, and feelings for Jasper, demanding I give them what they crave.

"Hey, baby." River bounds towards me. I catch her as she launches herself into my arms. I still haven't spoken to her about Michael; I'm trying to delay it until I have put the results in for Sammy.

"Hey, how are things?" I ask, squeezing her tight before releasing her. I sense Kyra's eyes on me and I'd be lying if I said it doesn't do things to me. This girl is changing me, making me feel.

"I'm okay. Sammy has been great and Mikey has been himself, really." She looks down to the floor and shrugs her shoulders before murmuring. "I know it's in me, Der, the fear from Danny and what he did." Her eyes lift to meet mine. "I just…" She sighs. "If he does share Danny's DNA, I want to know. The not knowing is making me crazy."

I pull her into me for another hug. "Riv, even if he does, it doesn't mean anything. He won't be like him. Danny was ill, River."

Sammy taps me on the shoulder and gestures for me to follow him out to the parking lot.

"Everything okay? Nothing unusual happen or no one loitering?" I ask, knowing he has been here since the call this morning.

"No, everything is normal, but I don't fucking like this. It's already making me edgy and has River questioning why I'm hanging around when I should be working."

He opens the boot of his car and slips me an envelope. "Here are the swabs you need. I need this done ASAP, Der." The look in his eyes is hard to decipher, but this has gone on long enough and they need to know one way or the other.

I say my goodbyes, taking Kyra by the hand and leading her to my car. The smile on River's face is a welcome sight.

* * * * *

Even in her casual dance wear, she's still unbelievably stunning. Her full lips purse into a kissable bow as she looks out the window and wrings her hands together in her lap. Her hair is pulled up off her elegant neck. I want to place kisses there and a bite mark. I shift to adjust my growing erection. I hear her inhale sharply as we pull up at her apartment.

I grab her wrist and turn her towards me. "What is it?" I follow her eyes as she looks over at a Mustang parked with the engine running. I pull my gun from its holster without needing her explanation; my intuition is telling me to find out who's in there.

"Wait here," I command as I exit the car.

I lock the doors and make my way across the road. The driver is not visible through the windscreen as he pulls out recklessly towards me. I faintly hear Kyra shouting, but I'm focused on reading the plates as he speeds past me.

I hear the door open and her light footsteps running towards me. "I knew there was something off with that car." She grips my arm. "I thought he was going to hit you there for a minute."

I grasp the nape of her neck, gently tilting her face to look up at me. "Kyra, why didn't you mention this today?"

Her eyes expand and her bottom lip disappears into her mouth before popping free, glistening with the moisture from her tongue. "I'm sorry, I wasn't sure if I was just being paranoid," she murmurs.

"I don't care if it's paranoia. I don't care if it's someone accidently brushing past you in the supermarket. I want to know about it!" I admonish, my tone leaving no room for argument. Her eyes drop to the floor. I grasp her with my other hand, the pads of my thumbs stroking her cheeks as I demand with my grip that she look at me. Her lashes flutter; her green beauties pierce me, nearly stealing my breath. "I care about you. Please, Kyra. I need to know all these things, little or big, okay?"

She tries to nod her head, but smiles when she can't move from my grasp. "Okay," she agrees; the promise in her tone and the look she gives me tells me she's being sincere. I bring my lips down to press them against her forehead.

"Give me your keys. Let me go in first just in case." I release her to go back to the car for her bag. I call Hans on my cell to run the plates and have a squad car stake out Kyra's apartment tonight in case the driver comes back.

Her place is empty and there's no sign of forced entry.

"It could just be my ex trying to scare me, Derek," she says, brushing past me to go to her bedroom.

Twenty minutes later, she emerges in a dress that hugs all her womanly curves, her full breasts are showcased in the low neckline. I travel down her toned legs until they end in a pair of heels I want her to have on with nothing else.

"Your cell."

I blink at her, confused.

"What?"

"Your cell phone is ringing." She giggles.

I shake my head and reach in my pocket to retrieve it. "Hans, what you got for me?"

"It's registered to a Matthew Winter. I ran his profile and he's deceased; died in a boating accident six months ago. I have his last known address if you want to check it out?"

"Yes, send it through." I hang up and pull Kyra back out of the apartment.

The drive back to my house is a tense one; my mind is on the case and who could be behind this. I checked the database for offenders I had a hand in putting away, but nothing came back to connect with this. I want Kyra staying at my place tonight. Tomorrow Sammy will spend the day with them again when I plan to follow the lead from the Mustang.

"Maybe it's too much. I don't get to dress up often." I look over at Kyra, picking up the back end of her conversation as I drive up to my house.

"I'm sorry, what?"

She flushes red. "The dress, I maybe overdressed for dinner."

I stop the car and put my finger up to her lips to hush her. "You look absolutely stunning. I'm honoured you would make such effort just for me." I brush her lip as I pull my hand away, feeling a satisfied spark igniting inside me when her breath catches. I open the car door and exit, coming around to help her out. I get a flash of her inner thigh as she steps out and it stirs the desire inside me. I'm beginning to ache to be between them.

Kyra

I watch as Derek starts to make dinner after handing me a glass of wine.

"This was my sister's speciality," he says. "She used to make it every Tuesday when our mom worked late."

Pain glosses his eyes as he mentions his sister; the word "sister" coming out a tone lower than every other word that leaves his mouth. The frost of grief tinges the atmosphere and dispels in the next moment when the front door opens and closes. Jasper's deep baritone voice fills the air, warming it with an electric pulse. It zaps through my veins and the emptiness leaves Derek's eyes.

"Der, that smells so good. You didn't tell me it was mac night, I have to…" His footsteps falter when his eyes rest upon me as he enters the kitchen.

"Hey," he says. The energy, like a natural being, manifests itself in the room, fogging my thoughts. His eyes rake over the dress I squeezed myself into, then they leave me and slowly assess Derek. "I didn't realise this was a date?" he questions, his voice sounding harsher than it should.

"It's not. It's just dinner, and you're welcome to join us," Derek practically growls in response. I watch them battle; a stare off that Derek wins. Jasper turns his gaze to me, pinning me with a smirk, which leaves me weightless and needing to reach for the counter for support.

"Okay, thanks. I'm starving, I haven't eaten all day," he chirps, grabbing an apple from the fruit bowl and taking a huge bite. His teeth break the skin, then crunch into the centre, the juices moisten his lips and a small droplet runs from the corner of his mouth; his tongue darts out to swipe it. I grip the counter and swallow hard. "You're blushing, Beauty." I turn my gaze to Derek's and see a swirl of heated caramel looking back at me. He called me *Beauty*. I feel like I could combust. Between the two of them, I'm already soaking my panties in need of a release I had never sought before. The ache built the longer Derek held my gaze. The fire had broken out all over my body.

"You're burning." Jasper's voice penetrates the haze and I reply with a whisper.

"Yes."

Derek smiles and drops his eyes to the pan that had begun to smoke. "It's fine. I caught it in time.*"*

Oh my God, he meant the dinner. I know the blush that now scorches my cheeks is completely visible to both of them. The smirks gracing their beautiful faces tell me as much. I follow Jasper to the dining area after a head gesture from Derek.

"So how is Hannah?" I ask, forcing her name past my lips. The atmosphere shifts at the mention of her name.

"She has some kind of bug. She's in bed trying to sleep it off. I had to pick her up baby safe medicine and I just came home to eat and grab an overnight bag. I don't want to leave her alone tonight."

It shouldn't matter. I've known all along nothing can ever happen between me and him, but the sting still pierces me.

Why can't logic control things instead of what the heart commands? Even if it gets shredded never gaining its desire.

"Wine, Beauty?" Derek's warm tone releases the tension taking over my body as he places a glass down in front of me. He's such a gentlemen, handsome and caring, but also commanding, successful, and confident. Everything I could want in a man, and I do want him, but the trouble is I want Jasper too, and just like the logic not standing a chance with the heart, it also doesn't stand up to want either. My body pulses with need just being in the same room as these two.

"How are things with the new garage?" Derek asks Jasper as he places the pot of food in the centre and takes a seat next to me. His thigh brushes mine, making me inhale sharply, then cough to hide my reaction to such a simple touch. Jasper's eyes burn through me from across the table like he senses the boil in my blood.

"It's good. Everything is set up. We'll be interviewing in the next few days." His gaze never leave mine and Derek's eyes never leave his as he speaks. I can't cope. I'm going to faint if I don't have some relief from them.

The relief comes from the ringing of Jasper's cell phone. "Hey, you okay? …It hasn't even been an hour, Hannah…Drink tap water… Fine, I'll buy some bottled and bring it …Okay now, I'm leaving." He finishes his call and stands. "I have to go. Thanks for dinner."

Derek squints his eyes. "You didn't get to eat any."

Jasper shrugs his shoulders. "She doesn't want to drink tap water while she's sick, so I need to get her some bottled."

I furrow my brow and look away from him. She already has him trained and under the thumb. He hadn't been gone an hour and she's calling him for an errand so silly. I can just imagine the hold she'll have on him when the baby comes.

She's the type to phase out everyone he spends time with, consume him, and mould him into her puppet.

Derek's hand covers mine, bringing me from my musing. "Eat, Beauty. I made this for you anyway." His smile made my own lips lift.

Jasper left without another word and the meal went down well, followed by a couple of glasses of wine. Derek put on some music while we emptied our plates and loaded the dish washer.

The wine works its way through my system, making me a little more relaxed than I would usually when alone in the company of a man. I can sense every time his eyes fall upon me and it sends a rush of excitement through my veins.

"Go relax in the lounge room," he whispers against my ear, making me shiver. I comply, leaving him to finish up.

I'm standing in front of the fireplace, looking at the pictures that adorn the mantel place. They're of Sammy, River, and Jasper with Michael in various stages of his young life. I feel Derek come up behind me, his heat crowding me, comforting me in a way I've never felt before.

I know once I take this step there's no going back. His pull is strong without any physical connection, so once I let him touch me, it will be an unstoppable force.

His hands grasp my hips, pulling me back against him. A gasp escapes my lips. His frame leans into me; his breath whispering against my ear. I feel his erection grow tall and proud against my ass cheeks and the nerves kick in with the adrenaline, making my body hum with a gentle shake. "I know you like him."

His words confuse me, then slam into me. He means Jasper. I try to step away from him, but his grip tightens. His nose nuzzles the hair away from my ear as his lips brush against the lobe. "He'll never leave her and give you anything you deserve, Kyra. He will marry her."

An emptiness opens up in my stomach at the words I know to be the truth. I decide in this moment to take a step I never thought I would have the confidence to take. I spin in his arms and crush my lips to his; the warmth engulfs me as he wraps his strong arms around me, lifting me from the floor. I climb his frame in needy erratic movements, my dress inching up my thighs and bunching at my waist. I know I'm exposed, but the heat of his crotch as his hard erection pushes against the wet satin of my panties only brings a groan from me.

The wine lowers my inhibitions and my lips welcome his as he prises mine apart and caresses my tongue with his own in a needy battle that he'll win with ease. His arms hold my thighs with no effort as he coaxes them to wrap further around his waist.

My hands pull on his hair. He walks us across the room, and I feel the cold press of the wall as Derek pins me to it and sends a shiver through my scorching body. His lips leave my mouth and travel down my neck to the valley of my breasts. My chest rises and falls in a needy rhythm, my breath escaping in pants.

"Damn, you're so beautiful, but we can't do this."

The heat and passion zaps from me like a camp fire having a gallon of iced water thrown on top of it. Realization and embarrassment make me want to throw up. I can't look up as I pull my dress down to cover my exposed panties.

"I'm sorry," I stutter, trying to compose myself.

I feel the warmth of his hand as he grasps my chin, tilting my head back, so my eyes meet the fire in his. "Don't be sorry, Beauty. I loved every second of having your body against mine, the soft touch of your lips on mine. I just know you've been drinking and I don't want to get carried away when there is no rush, baby. And there is no way I want to waste our touches in a drunken haze."

I nod my head as he releases me from his grasp. "Okay, you're right," I agree. "I should grab a cab."

The breath leaves me as I'm re-pinned back against the wall, his heavy frame consuming my smaller one. "Stay. Sleep in my shirt and just stay. Wake up and have coffee with me, please," he asks, but it sounds like a plea. His lips gently press against the sensitive area just below my ear and tingles assault my skin, leaving goose bumps as the proof of his effect on my body.

"Okay," I whisper, pushing my body into his.

His lips find mine again briefly before pulling away. "God, I need to shower. Come with me. I'll get you a shirt to sleep in."

I follow him up the stairs to his room. It's masculine; the walls are the colour of slate, the furniture sleek and stylish, and a huge four poster bed is the focal point.

He walks over to a dresser, opening a drawer and pulling a shirt free, handing it to me. "I need to shower. Did you want to shower?" he asks. Tension builds and my body gently quivers. *Oh God, we will be naked, together. Would he want…?*

"Your own shower, Beauty." He chuckles. "I told you I don't want to do anything like that with you yet. Not until you're completely coherent so you can remember every place I touch you." He steps forward, his lips hovering near mine. "And I will be everywhere. There is not an inch on this perfect, beautiful body you won't feel me. I'll leave you hypersensitive and aching in the most delicious of ways."

My nipples peak as they brush against his chest with my

needy uneven breaths.

He slips past me, leaving me lightheaded. I feel like I could orgasm from just his words. "Beauty," he calls holding out his hand. I walk to him and grasp the hand he offers, letting him lead me across the hall to a new room. The room is completely cream everywhere—the walls, the carpet, the furniture—and it's airy and feminine.

"This was River's favourite room. She said it was soothing. She used to come in here to read." He points over at the bookshelf loaded with books. I walk over and brush my hand across the spines, stopping and pulling out, *Denying Heaven*. A smile snakes across my lips at the title; fitting really, considering I was denying my body a release it desperately yearned for.

"The bathroom is through there. I'll be back to check on you when I've showered."

I watch him stride from the room and exhale the breath I'd been holding in. My body is on the edge of explosion. I drop the book onto the bed and slip my dress down, leaving me in my strapless bra and panties. I check the door and hear the shower running from across the hall in Derek's room.

I kick off my heels and lay back on the soft mattress; it's pure luxury compared to mine at my apartment, which was there when I moved in. My skin is hyper aware of every subtle brush against it. I slip my hand into my panties and gasp at the contact; I'm wet and swollen as I rub the pads of my fingers up and down the folds, letting my arousal coat my fingers before I slip them inside.

Derek

 Leaving her all flustered and burning up for me was so tough; the fact I had been reining myself in from fucking the life out of Jasper on so many occasions helped my self-control massively. When I had her tiny, little body writhing against me downstairs, her heat grinding against my erection, it nearly had me losing control. Her inexperienced hands and tongue attacking me in a burst of lust was one of the hottest things I've ever experienced and in the moment, I had completely shut out the emotions, the craving for Jasper, and the grief of my sister's death that still haunts me. I felt only her.

 I was in the moment until I broke away, then like a tidal wave he crashed back into me, flooding me with want; a desire rooted so deep I can almost feel him when he isn't there. Craving him has become a part of me. He lives inside me and I'll never sate that, but maybe I can ease it with her.

 I turn the shower on before undressing. I'm about to step in when I remember there are no products in her bathroom so I wrap a towel around my waist and grab some of the extra wash and shampoo to take her in case she wanted to shower.

 I get to the entrance of the room she's staying in, and my

legs nearly give way from under me, my stomach flipping over. A sliver of soft light cast across the hall gives me a view through the gap into her room. I see her; she's lying on the bed, her deep red hair fanned out across the cream sheets, her tanned bare skin on show for my private viewing. I feel like I should walk away like I'm invading her privacy, but when her hand slips into her panties I can't look away and my cock tents the towel, demanding attention. Her soft pants fill the still air, her chest rising with every breath, her nipples peaking, the white lace bra she has on barely covering her breasts.

"Ohhh," she moans. I have to lean against the frame to keep me steady. Her hand moving up and down more rapidly increases her moans. She's writhing on the bed and her face is so stunning in the height of passion. "Derek…oh Jasper."

She groans as she reaches her peak. Hearing my name and his leave her lips in an orgasm has me coming undone and I turn and hurry back to my room, stripping the towel and entering the shower. I fist my hard as steel cock and pump my shaft a few times before the string of white come decorates the shower wall in an intense release, nearly bringing me to my knees.

When I'm able to catch my breath and steady my weak limbs, I wash and dress in a casual shirt and sweats. I chance a look through the gap left by her door not being fully closed and see she's put my shirt on and is asleep with a book on her stomach. I don't risk going in. Instead I go to bed and dream of her and Jasper together with me watching them.

Jasper

I didn't want to leave them. Just seeing her in our kitchen, so at ease and comfortable with Derek left me jealous, but I wasn't sure of the cause. Maybe it was the way Derek looked at her and the fact he was cooking his sister's dish. He had only ever cooked that for me; it was special to him and took effort from him not to break every time he prepared it. Yet, he made it for Kyra.

It was such a relief leaving Hannah's to walk into mine and Derek's home, and have Kyra's presence fill it. It made me want things I had never before even entertained. The thoughts of how different it would be if she was the girl I got pregnant instead of Hannah.

I stop by the grocery store to pick up bottled water and make my way back to Hannah's apartment. The drowning, suffocating feeling overwhelms me as I enter. I have to stop and take a few deep breaths; I can't believe how lonely and wrong this feels. How can I live like this from now on? Twenty-eight and already miserable before the ring's even on my finger.

"Hey." Hannah's voice brings my attention to her. She

stands in black lace underwear and nothing else, her hair all straightened and her face done up with girly shit.

"What's going on?" I ask, confused by her turn around.

She saunters towards me, her hips swaying, trying to be seductive. "I know this isn't ideal for you, Jasper, but we had a lot of fun in the bedroom. There's no reason we still can't. I'm going to be your wife; I want you to have all the perks that come with that." Her tits push against my chest as she stands on her tiptoes to plant a kiss to my lips.

"Hannah what the fuck? You said you were ill. I left dinner for this?"

Her eyes narrow. She pulls back and then does something I never thought I would ever witness. Tears form in her eyes and flow down her cheeks.

Her chest heaves, making a horrid sound rip from her. "I'm gross already, I know it and it's just going to get worse," she wails between breaths. She hiccups and red blotches spring up on her face. "I know you won't stick around. You already hate me. I'm gross and you don't want me, and no one else will with a kid in tow and I'll be alone to do it all while you slut it up with all the girls who aren't pregnant and gross!"

I go to her and swipe the wet from her now red cheeks. "You're not gross and I'm not going anywhere. That's my kid you're carrying, that means you get me. Now stop being dramatic."

Her hands push my chest. "I'm not being dramatic. My own boyfriend doesn't want to touch me. I have a right to get upset," she sobs and my stomach coils. She's right, I don't want to touch her. Kyra floats into my mind and then an image of her and Derek. I shake my head and grab Hannah's hips, pulling her into me. I crush my lips with hers and then swoop her into a bridal hold, carrying her into the bedroom. Her hungry kisses do nothing for me and I have to concentrate on thinking of Kyra and Derek making out to sustain my erection.

"Jasper, I need to feel you so bad," she pants as I place her on the bed. She undoes her bra, freeing her tits, her rosy nipples standing proud, but doing nothing for me, not even a fucking twitch. I feel no desire to suck, pinch, or bite them.

Fuck, I'm broken. Derek and his weird cryptic mood shifts and Kyra's sexy fucking dress have broken me.

Hannah lunges forward and unbuttons my jeans. I can't look at her as I replace her face with Kyra's and as I feel her petite hand free my erection, my thoughts stay with Kyra. I feel like a prick thinking of Kyra in this way, which is also fucking new. Since when did I care who I fantasised about? But I can't help the want I have for her and the emotions niggling at the parts of me, trying to warm the cold. I know I'll never be able to have her, so what's wrong with a little fantasy; everyone does that, right? I imagine it's her soft lips and warm mouth sucking the tip of my cock. It's her hand jerking me off as her tongue tastes the tip.

I grip her head as Kyra's green eyes looking up at me flood my mind. "Fuck." I push my dick in deeper and Kyra's image flashes to Derek's. I push deeper and then jolt back.

Derek! What the fuck?

I watch Hannah jump from the bed and dart towards the bathroom, heaving. I'm still standing there trying to reason with my thought process.

"God, Jasper. I'm pregnant. My gag reflex is twice as bad now," she grumbles and lies down on the bed. "I can't do sex now. Can you get me some water?"

I comply, zipping my dick back in my pants and hurrying from the room.

Derek

I make a pot of coffee and scramble some eggs. Knowing Kyra was asleep across the hall, wearing my shirt and nothing else, tested my restraint last night. I was angry at Jasper for dropping us and running back to Hannah while just sitting down to eat, and it brought back the realization that he'll be married and have a child soon. I'm waiting for the time he'll tell me he's moving out. I know it's coming and it's eating away at me. I hate that I want him and feel so much for him, but can never express that in the way I want to.

    I sense the change in the way he is with me and I swear he wants me too, but it could be my mind playing tricks on me—hope manifesting something that isn't true. I need to concentrate on what's in front of me, wanting me. I know Kyra has it bad for Jasper, but I see her want for me too and I'm the one who can give her something in return, something more than sex if I just try and let myself feel for someone else. If I can push past the guilt and let myself have a small sliver of happiness, maybe we can heal the hole Jasper will leave in us.

    I hear Jasper's heavy foot falls carry up the lobby, and I check my watch. 7:45 a.m. He's home early. He enters without making eye contact and looks guilty as hell.

"Hey," I greet him, and pour him a cup of coffee.

He nods his head, taking the mug and still not looking at me as Kyra's small body comes into view at the door way. She's in my shirt and it comes midway down her toned, tanned thighs; her red, mussed hair looks gorgeous all messed up from bed, her face clear of all make up. She's stunning.

The sound of something smashing makes me jolt.

"Fuck," Jasper says as he hops back from the dark river of coffee covering the tiles heading towards his feet. "Fuck, I'm clumsy. I dropped it."

Kyra bites her lip and looks between us both. I point to the cupboard where we keep the mop and broom, and follow a retreating Jasper from the kitchen and up the stairs.

I follow him to his room where he paces. "What was that?" I ask.

"Did you fuck her?"

I stride towards him, pointing my finger at him. "Watch your mouth, Jasp," I warn. "And what does it matter to you anyway?"

He scrubs his hands down his face, then up through his hair, shaking his head. "It doesn't, it doesn't. Fuck, it shouldn't."

I grab his arm and force him to look at me. "I like her. We kissed. She drank too much and slept in the spare room, not that any of this should matter. Did you fuck Hannah last night?" I ask before leaving him standing there staring at my back as I exit.

As I step out of his room, Kyra exits the room she stayed in. She must have followed me up. She's back in her dress from last night, and she offers a timid smile

"Hey, I just... I need to go home to change before work."

"Okay, I'll take you."

* * * * *

The car is filled with a tense atmosphere; the relaxed, happy girl from last night has been replaced with the timid, almost nervous Kyra sitting in the passenger seat, twirling a strand of hair around her finger.

"You okay?" I chance a quick glance at her before returning my eyes to the road.

"Yeah, I'm fine. I just think..." She shifts in her seat, turning her body towards me.

"I don't really know what's happening with us. I'm grateful you stopped me from going too far last night. I drank more wine than I'm used to…Not that I regret anything that did happen …I just mean—"

I reach a hand out to grasp hers.

"We can just go slow and see what happens. Let's not overthink anything right now." I smile and pull up at her apartment. The squad car I requested is parked outside and the officer gets out and approaches us.

"Detective." He nods his head at me.

"Anything to report?" I ask, quirking a brow.

"Nothing, sir. A neighbour, a female, came in at around one a.m. and there's been no activity since."

I nod my head at him and guide Kyra inside with a hand on her lower back. Her place is as we left it.

"Go do what you need to do, Beauty, and pack a bag. I want you to stay with me until this is resolved."

"But we don't know how long that will be."

I bite down the need to demand she does as she's told out of my own fear that this is all about me and I want her to be near me at all times so I can protect her.

"Just stay a few days for now." I close the distance, reaching up to stroke her cheek. "For my peace of mind, just stay a few days."

She bites down on her bottom lip and it's sexy as sin. I swallow the saliva coating my mouth and step away from her.

"Go change." I nod in the direction of her room, my voice hoarse from the arousal she caused from simply biting her lip.

I check my emails on my phone; the address for the registered Mustang is only an hour away; that will be my first stop today. I need something, any lead on this guy. Not knowing the motive or confirmed pattern of this unsub is leaving me anxious. I check a text from Sammy, informing me he'll be staying at the studio until noon, then Jasper will be there until closing.

"Ready," Kyra chimes from behind me. I smile at the sight of her in her dancewear. This woman can pull off any outfit. She would be the death of me if I had to watch her dance around all day in this skin tight outfit.

"What's wrong?" she asks, reaching up to smooth out the crease from my forehead. The thoughts of Jasper being there all afternoon, watching her doing that exact thing makes me have conflicting feelings. I'm not sure if I'm jealous of him getting to watch her, or her having him watch her. This is all becoming a mess. How can this ever work out? I know he has a thing for her, and I have one for them both and she seems to have one for both of us. It's bound to cause trouble later down the line. Jasper is already jealous.

"I need to go now. I don't want to be late. River

promoted me, and she's informing the girls today that she's pregnant and that I'll be taking on the general running of the day to day stuff." She beams, and I clasp her hand and walk her back to my car.

* * * * *

I pull up to the small detached house—the address of the Mustang. The lawn is well kept; there's a rocking chair on the porch, and an older lady is rocking back and forth.

"Hello," she greets, coming to a stop, the weariness evident in her posture.

I pull my badge and smile as warmly as I can manage.

"Hello, ma'am. I'm detective Jefferson. Have you got a few minutes to answer some questions?"

She rises to her feet and leans in to check my badge.

"What's this about?"

"We're investigating the owner of a car that came up registered to this address, ma'am. A Mustang."

She holds her hand up to stop me.

"That was my son's. He passed away and I sold it on, I couldn't look at it, knowing he would never be home to drive it."

I slip my badge away.

"I'm sorry for your loss. Can you tell me who it was sold to?"

"He told me his name was Ethan." She puts her finger to her lip and looks up to the sky. "No, Evan. He told me he would sort all the paperwork, so I wouldn't need to worry, and paid me in cash." She takes a step towards me. "He was a handsome young man, seemed pleasant. Is he okay?"

An uneasy chill races up my spine at the name Evan.

"Can you describe him?"

"Blond, handsome features, about your height, in his early thirties if I was to guess."

It could just be a coincidence, but the cold ice flooding my veins and the description told me it was Mya's ex, Evan. Could he be behind this?

The memories of Mya's death and the circumstances leading up to her suicide fill my head in a torrent of images and a painful ache of grief on the drive back to the station. Evan was Mya's first and only love. He was older than her, and he was controlling. First was her image; she would no longer wear skirts or dresses. They were replaced with sweaters, even in the summer heat. I noticed she became timid, nothing like the outgoing girl she once was. When I first saw her bruises by chance when she was pulling on a sweater, the brother, man, and agent in me knew straight away what was happening. She finally broke and told me these weren't the first marks he had left her with. The brother's rage won the battle and I confronted him with threats. If he ever came near her again, I would kill him. He punished her for telling me by sleeping with her best friend, filming it, and sending it to her. The thing about love, especially first love when it's with someone who abuses you, it makes it hard to see that you're in fact a victim of a crime. It's not always the violence that does the damage. It's the physiological effect it has. It clouds judgement; the abuser infects you like a virus, pollutes your mind, and takes away your rationality. They corrupt your thoughts by making you think you owe them, that to love them means accepting them, standing by them why they try to change. They convince you that you must have done something wrong to make them abuse you in the first place. They're a poison that strips you of everything you once were. Despite all he had done, she was brainwashed into loving him. That video crippled her, broke her fragile psyche and heart, making her take her own life. She plunged to her death from a cliff's edge. I was on duty the night the call came in. I remember driving there, feeling sorry for the family of whoever this person was, to have to tell them that this person killed themselves when all they would hear was that their loved one had gotten so low, had nowhere to turn, that rather than go on living, they threw themselves off a cliff. When I pulled up to other squad cars and yellow tape, a friend and fellow officer rushed towards my patrol car with tears in his eyes, shaking his head. A hole opened up in my chest. I stepped out to be pushed against the car with force by him.

"It's Mya, man. Oh, God. I'm so sorry, Der, it's Mya."

I remember the words and my pushing at him to let me pass, but more officers hands gripped me, holding me back.

"It's not fucking Mya! What are you talking about? Let me pass! It's not Mya. She wouldn't. It's not my baby sister, you bastards! Let me pass!" I screamed until my throat was raw, my legs buckled and grief attacked every part of my soul. No physical pain can compare to the emotional pain of grief. Our mother blamed me for her death. She blamed me for interfering with Evan. She couldn't even look at me at Mya's funeral. Evan dropped off the map. I was informed by Mya's best friend that she was heartbroken. He broke her down and made her end her life. I wanted his life in my hands. I wanted to feel his pulse slow and fade to nothing as I ended his life. I never saw him again.

* * * * *

I find Hans in my office when I get there.

"You know it's a conflict of interest, having her stay with you."

I throw my keys on the desk and scowl at him.

"Why would you think she's staying with me?"

"Peters, the officer who staked out her place last night, said she didn't come home and you brought her back this morning. I may not be as a good a detective as you, but I don't need to be to know she stayed with you."

"She's staying with River. I just drive her where she needs to be. She doesn't have a car and I don't need to explain shit to you." I jab him with a finger in the chest. "This is personal, Hans. I think this is aimed at me." I walk around the desk, taking a seat and powering up my computer. "I need you to find me everything from the last year on Evan Mills."

His hands come down on the desk, his frame leaning towards me.

"Why do I know that name, and how is this connected to you?"

"He was Mya's boyfriend and I think he's the one doing this. I think it's to send me a message."

Hans lets out a gush of air and rubs his hand over his face. "Why would he have grievance with you and after so long?"

The cold freeze that had set into my veins is replaced with a hot boil. I spring to my feet, sending my chair flying backwards and crashing into the wall with a loud thump.

"I don't fucking know! Perhaps he, like my mother, blames me for Mya. What I do know is I want him found so I can KILL THE SON OF A BITCH!" I roar, hammering my fist onto my desk, making Hans flinch.

"I'll go run his profile now." He turns and leaves.

I want this bastard caught, so he doesn't hurt anyone else

to get to me. Why not just be a fucking man and come after me? I grow more frustrated by the second. My phone pulls me from the spiral of anger, frustration, guilt and irritation I'm beginning to drown in. Jasper's name flashing on my screen makes me sigh. I need to hear his voice. I need comfort; that isn't something I'm used to needing, but God dammit, I'm a mess inside and I need a reassuring presence right now.

"Hey." His warm tone echoes down the line.

"Hey, everything okay?" I hear him moving around and I know he's brushing a hand through his messy hair.

"Yeah, listen I'm sorry about this morning. I just had a bad night and took it out on you." Static hums through the line before he speaks again.

"We had a crisis at the studio."

My body tenses and scenarios of what possible crisis they've had rush through my mind like snippets from a movie trailer.

"What happened?" I sound breathless. I feel dizzy. Memories flood my mind from when Danny changed all our lives on the night he lost it and kidnapped River: Sammy's frantic rambles as I found him shot and desperate to find River, Jasper being wheeled out unconscious from a near fatal stomach wound where Danny shot him. Than locating him, confronting him, and being left for dead, bleeding into the dirt. What if something happened to one of them? How would we cope after everything we've been through? How can we cope with another psycho targeting one us?

"Der? Der? Fuck, did I lose signal again?" Jasper's voice pulls me back from my memories.

"I'm here. What happened?"

"Oh, Mikey had an inset day, so River brought him to the studio. Sammy told him off for running his cars along the mirrors, next thing, Mikey runs off to the bathroom and water starts pissing out the door, flooding the hall. Sent River into her head again." I hear him exhale. "Anyway, she closed the studio early, that's why I'm calling. Kyra said she's staying at our place?"

"Actually yeah, just take her back there. I'll talk with you tonight; make sure I'm home before you leave."

"I'm staying home tonight. Hannah has gone on some city trip to look at dresses."

I stop myself from punching the wall and grind my teeth, biting out, "Fine. See you tonight, then."

I don't wait for a reply.

Kyra

Watching River break down and cry was disturbing to witness. She's such a strong woman and to see her fall apart pulled on my emotions. I don't know the whole story about what she went through, but I know from the news articles that six years ago her then boyfriend was abusing her, murdered people including her father, and attempted to murder Sammy, Jasper, and Derek. He then came back for River nearly a year later and she killed him.

This was something I had never lived or been around. My life was curfews and church on a Sunday; I can't even imagine myself going through what she has and surviving every day, getting up and living a normal life.

I wasn't sure what caused River's overreaction to Mikey's bad behavior, but something was troubling her.

Jasper sent her home with Sammy and Mikey, and then stayed to help clean the mess and lock up.

I'm now back in the cream room at Derek's, freshly showered in sweats and a sweater. I just want some cocoa and to go back to Denying Heaven; I would rather live in Bulk's heartache and love problems than my own right now. Fictional men have always been a better option for me. I shake my head at my own pathetic past with men—or man—in my case.

"Hey, I made dinner," Jasper calls though the closed door. I open It to find him leaning against the frame. He's still in his jeans and shirt from earlier; the dark blue is a sexy contrast with the light cobalt of his eyes, his mussed hair even more messy than usual. He holds a pizza box, the pepperoni and cheese scent rising from it with the steam. My stomach growls in approval. Junk food is perfect for the mood I'm in.

"Made dinner, huh?" I raise a brow.

His smirk isn't getting any easier to ignore; he is stunning—should be gracing billboards stunning.

"I made the call." He wiggles the hand braced against the frame. I see his cell in his hand and smile, grabbing the box from him before I race down the stairs. "Run all you like, Beautiful, there's no way that body can consume all that pizza."

I turn half way down the stairs and grin. "This body burns calories at a rapid rate from dancing every day, therefore I can consume them at a rapid rate, too." I hold up the box. "This is a medium Pepperoni Passion, next time XL this bad boy!" I chuckle and continue my race to the couch.

"Soda?" Jasper smiles, walking in to the room and placing sodas on the side table next to me. I was already devouring the first slice and preparing for another. The cushion dips next to me, then his warmth presses all up my side as he takes the seat next to me. He sits too close; my stomach has turned into a spinning top, the slight brush of his arm against mine has chills racing through me, leaving a trail of goose bumps in their wake.

"Xbox?" he asks, picking up the remote and pointing it towards a huge flat screen. I struggle to push the last bite of pizza down my now dry throat.

I grab the soda and guzzle it, trying to coat my mouth, so I can answer him. "I don't know how," I murmur.

He beams at me, then winks. "Well, I'm a fantastic teacher in all things, darling. Grab a controller." He points to a console under the TV.

Derek

Nothing! That's what Hans brought me. Evan was AWOL; his parents hadn't seen or heard from him in years. He's dropped off the map, not so much as a parking ticket flagged. He's a ghost, and I'm the motherfucker he is haunting.

I called Sammy to ask if Kyra could stay with them until this was resolved, and to tell River Kyra had had a break-in and was looking for a new place. It wasn't a complete lie; she will be getting a new place, she just doesn't know it yet.

I get out of the car once I'm home and mentally prepare myself for seeing both Kyra and Jasper inside. I turn the handle and the front door opens. Rage from Jasper's stupidity furies my already frayed nerves.

I march through the lobby to find him and Kyra laughing and fucking around on his Xbox.

"What the fuck is wrong with you? DID YOU LEARN NOTHING FROM DANNY?" I holler, startling Kyra.

Jasper jumps to his feet, throwing his controller on the couch. "What the fuck is your problem now?" He squares his shoulders and scowls at me as I step forward into him.

Our chests touch and I grasp the back of his neck and lean into his face. "The front door just opened. I could have been anybody. Do you remember what happened here when Danny came for River?" He looks down at the floor and I have to release him as the anger is replaced with the usual burning lust. My cock is growing rapidly in my slacks and my breathing becomes uneven and deep.

"Well, I was here with her, so don't get all in my face. It won't happen again. I'm going to shower," Jasper says, walking past me and nudging me with his shoulder. I turn from Kyra's gaze, so she doesn't see the bulge in my pants. When is he going to stop having this effect on me?

Nimble fingers touch my shoulder. "Hey. Bad day?"

"Yeah. I'm sorry you just witnessed that, Beauty." I take a few deep breaths and turn, pulling her petite form into mine and wrap my arms around her. I inhale her scent and burrow my nose into her neck. She smells sweet, edible. I feel my cock stir again and groan. I pull away and smile down at her. "I'm going to shower."

She nods her head, strands of red fall from her up-do, caressing her cheek. "Okay, I was going to go to bed and read."

I reach out to push the loose stands behind her ear. "Okay, come on then." I clasp her hand, pulling her behind me to the stairs. I get to the top and falter, her tiny frame crashes against mine and I hear her gasp.

Jasper turns, completely naked, and holds up a bottle of shampoo as he comes out of my room. "I took mine to Hannah's. You don't mind, do you? Or are you going to bust my balls for this too?"

I can't speak. The hard on I was fighting downstairs has come back full force and is almost painful. He is fucking perfect. He huffs at me and shakes his head before going to his room, his ass on display as he does; the muscles in his back flexing with each step. "Night," I choke out, dropping Kyra's hand and rushing to my room.

Jasper

I knew he was right about the front door and the alarms being off. I was foolish and too wrapped up in Kyra's presence to think about anything else. When Hannah told me her mother was taking her away for a couple of days, the relief nearly overwhelmed me; the pressure of having to marry her was having a depressing effect on me. I feel like I'm in quicksand and nothing is in my control; life really kicks you in the balls sometimes and unfortunately some people a lot more than once.

Just being in Kyra's presence is soothing. She makes me relax and feel like I can be me; the me only Sammy, River, and Derek get to see. She's funny and cute, she's never judgmental, and she doesn't scrunch her nose when I swear, or roll her eyes when I ordered us pizza for dinner. She's useless at Call of Duty and kept shooting me, but it was cute as fuck; the faces she would pull, her tongue coming out when she thought she was doing well.

Derek coming in and shouting at me killed the happy buzz I had been in for the first time in… I don't know how long. My head is a mess. Nothing makes sense lately. I needed to get away from him and shower to take care of the hard on I had been sporting since seeing Kyra moving around the studio in cropped lycra legging things. It only got harder when Derek fucking grabbed me like some dominant asshole. It was just the sexual tension left over from Kyra, and I just needed to take care of it in the shower.

I stripped off and remembered I had taken all my toiletries and shit to Hannah's. Coming back from Derek's room with his shampoo and finding him and Kyra hand in hand, coming up the stairs and looking like deer caught in the headlights. Looking back at them would have almost been funny if I wasn't so turned on by the fact they were both biting their lips. I know Der was just stopping himself from shouting at me again after neither of them said a word. I left them to watch my bare ass go back to my room.

The spray from the shower beat against my skin in tiny hot pellets. Gripping my full dick, I stroke the shaft; Kyra's face comes into view behind my closed eyes and I pump harder into my fist, my balls tightening, my chest heaving, making my breathing ragged. I imagine her biting her lip, then dropping to her knees. "Fuck yeah, Kyra. Open that mouth for me baby, swallow my come," I groan, her vision morphing to Derek's. I feel the tingle in my spine, then my dick explodes its release with an intensity so strong my knees buckle.

"What the fuck?!" I'm just tired and still thinking about the argument. That's all this is.

* * * * *

The next few days passed in a haze of strained encounters. Der had already left and took Kyra with him the next morning when I came down. He had brewed the coffee and left a note saying he would be working late and that Kyra had the day off, so was spending it with River. When he did come back, he hardly spoke to me; he was on edge. I would sense his eyes on me when he thought I wasn't paying attention; it was tense and confusing as fuck.

I tried to bring up the case, but he bit my head off and stormed out of the room. I had been spending my days interviewing for the new business and swapping shifts at Twinkle Toes with Sammy. Being around Kyra helped release some of the pent up stress I felt.

It's now day four. Hannah has prolonged her trip and I couldn't be happier about that. It's Sammy's little brother, Jase's, birthday and we're having a barbecue at our house for him, just the family. Kyra and River are at the studio. Der has a uniformed officer staking the place out, so Sammy can go pick Jake up, and me and Der can get the place ready, well-stock the beer fridge and buy the meat.

I bring out the plates and shit he asked me to go inside to get, no please or fuck all; he's beginning to grind on my last nerve. I step onto the patio and see him pacing with his phone pressed to his ear. He nods, and the furrow of his brow and hand on his hip tell me he's either relieved or worried about whatever he's being told; whatever it is, it looks personal. I place the stuff down on the table and walk over to him.

He ends the call and gives me a fleeting smile. "I need to go to the station."

He starts to walk past me, but I stop him, seizing his arm. He looks down to where my hand holds him, then to my eyes. "It's Jase's birthday. River will need you here today, can't this wait?"

He reaches down and pries my hand from his arm. "No."

Kyra

I smile over at River showing Amy, a dance student learning a routine for her college audition, how to extend her reach with her leg lifts, and then smile down to Mikey who also watches River.

Staying at River's has given me an insight to Mikey's increased bad behaviour. The lack of respect for Sammy's authority is a new development, apparently, and he's growing more disobedient every day.

"Mikey, grab mommy her bottle of water," River asks him, pointing to her bottle.

"You look pale, are you feeling alright?" I stand and walk towards her.

Mikey comes over with her water and drops the bottle at her feet.

"Pick it up and pass it to me, Mikey. Now please," she commands him. He just stares back at her. "Fine." She leans down her, weight shifting, a soft whimper escaping her as she collapses at my feet.

Amy lets out a startled cry and rushes towards us. I drop to my knees and gather her head to rest on my thighs as I check her pulse, which is a little faster than it should be. Her eyes flutter open, her pupils dilating. "What happened?"

"You fainted. How do you feel?" I reach for the bottle of water and help her sit up and sip some.

"Where's Mikey?" she breathes. I check behind me and notice he's gone. I look up at Amy and she shrugs.

River gets to her feet and I follow suit, steadying her when she sways. "Mikey!" she calls.

We walk out into the corridor and see him sitting under the reception desk, and I crawl down to sit with him. "Hey, Mikey, Come on, its okay. Mommy's fine. Look she's right there." I coax him out from under the desk to point to River leaning against the wall a few feet away

"I need the bathroom. Mikey, can you get mommy some water and wait here for me?"

Mikey nods. River looks to me and I see the worry in her eyes. She holds her hand out to me; I slip my arm behind her back and guide her to the bathroom and into a cubicle.

She slips her pants down and I turn to give her some privacy. "Ky," she croaks. I turn to see blood on the tissue she's holding. "I need you to drive me to the hospital." Tears form and spill onto her cheeks.

I swallow the lump in my throat, and help her stand and pull up her bottoms. I can't imagine what she must be feeling, but I'm scared and worried for her; all this upset with Mikey is clearly having an effect on her health. I just hope she'll open up and tell me what's happening with them, so I can understand and comfort her if needed. Mikey waits with Amy when we come out and he hands River a bottle of water.

"Amy, would you ring the students' parents that are due in for the late class and let them know we had an emergency and it's cancelled. All the numbers are in the folders, and ring Dawn too. Let her know we won't be needing her to assist tonight. Then lock the door as you leave." I grab my bag and hand her the spare set of keys. She nods her head and turns her worried gaze to River.

"Let's go, Mikey."

"Wait. My bag." River says. "You'll have to drive. My keys are in my bag."

I smile and snatch up her bag. I hate driving and told people I couldn't just so no one ever asked me too. I rarely do it, but this isn't about me. I need to get River to the hospital. If she loses this baby, it'll be devastating for her and Sammy, and impact all the lives I had come to care about.

When we arrive at the emergency room they ask River to fill in an insurance form. I stare daggers at the receptionist, but she seems oblivious to the fact.

"I really think you should call Sammy," I say, although River still looks dazed.

Michael shakes his head, tears in his eyes. "He won't love me no more if you tell him. I'm not like him. I swear I'm not."

I reach for him, swiping at the tears. "Who, sweetie? Who are you not like?"

The little sobs that come from him make his frame tremble and I pull him into a hug, my own body struggling to keep my emotions for spewing out. My heart aches for him. "He won't love me like Mommy doesn't. Mom cries to Dad about that man being my real dad. She says I'm like him and his mom stopped loving him and that he done really bad things because he was evil." He stutters between sobs. My insides have coiled; every maternal instinct in me is humming with need to comfort him.

"Calm down," I say, softly. He hyperventilates and River holds a hand over her mouth, shaking her head. Her tears bring forth my own. The agony in her eyes from what she's hearing is soul breaking to witness.

She grabs Mikey from my grasp and crushes him to her chest. Her strong overpowering love for her child emanates from her in waves.

"Mommy loves you baby. I would never stop loving you. I didn't mean those things. You weren't supposed to hear that stuff, baby. I'm sorry, and I love you."

"I was projecting my fears and he was just reacting to them," River mumbles. Mikey has fallen asleep in the chair next to her bed. Dehydration, the doctor said, and spotting are normal in some pregnancies. She's healthy, just needs to drink more. We both cried and hugged when the doctor gave her the results.

"Ma'am, there's a Detective Jefferson outside demanding I let him through."

My eyes bulge as do River's. "Yeah let him in," she says.

"How did he know?" she asks.

"Because it's my job to know this stuff, Riv, and I shouldn't need other means of finding this shit out. What happened and why didn't you call someone?" Derek asks, skimming past me to stroke River's hair.

"I'm fine. I fainted. Dehydration." She shrugs. "I actually feel fine since they put this in." She holds up her hand with the drip in to hydrate her. "I can leave soon; they're just doing the discharge papers."

Derek looks over to Mikey. "I'll take Mikey back to my place, to Jasp, and come back for you two."

"I can drive us to your house," I speak up, raising my hand like a child. He holds such authority, I actually feel like one sometimes; I think we all do when in his presence.

He looks between River and me and nods. "Okay, great. I'm guessing by the fact he hasn't called me and isn't here, Sammy doesn't know about this?" He narrows his eyes at River and she squirms.

"I didn't want to worry him with more stuff until I had to."

"Fair enough."

My mouth pops open and River's is a mirror image of mine. "Really? No lecture?"

He folds his arms, making the muscles bunch his suit jacket. "I agree that sometimes it's best to keep things from those we love if it's in their best interests." She eyes him suspiciously. He drops his arms and collects Mikey up, leaving us.

Derek

I got a call from Hans while setting up the barbecue to tell me they found the car and driver of the Mustang. It was involved in a car accident and the driver fits the description of the suspect from the lady who sold the car. But according to his driving licence, it says he is Matthew Roy. They found notes in the glove box that matched the ones found at the scenes of the crimes, but the driver is in critical condition and can't be questioned. I needed to see him; I needed to see if it was Evan going by a different name.

I didn't know what I wanted more: for it to be him and finally have him in front of me, or for it to be just a coincidence that I knew these women and these were random acts with no one but the sick fuck to blame for the crimes he inflicted.

I left things even more strained with Jasper and I hate the way things are between us at the moment, but know it's my doing.

When I got to the hospital and saw that it wasn't Evan, I was a little relieved. I wasn't responsible for these victims, after all. I didn't recognise this guy; his name was never in my arrest files. This was just coincidence.

"Officer Greer, who was watching Twinkle Toes, is outside. He said he couldn't get your cell, but he followed your girls here," Hans says behind me.

My stomach hits the floor and I swear my vision clouds. "What?"

"It's okay, I found out from the nurse they're both okay, but she couldn't share more details than that."

I push past him into the corridor and locate a nurse, demanding they take me to them. I ask Hans and Greer not to leave the hospital until River and Kyra have left.

Mikey jumps from the car as soon as I pull up, he seems in high spirits which is a vast contrast to the last couple of weeks. I follow him into the house, and go through to the patio and find the birthday banner up, the barbecue set, and everything ready.

"Humph, woo buddy!" Jasper stutters, catching Mikey as he leaps into his arms. "Hey," he coos, stroking his hair.

I feel relaxed for the first time in weeks. Jasper's eyes find mine. "How come you've got Mikey?"

I open my mouth to speak, but quickly close it at the commotion of Sammy coming in with Jase. We don't get to see him as often as everyone would like and each time he seems to grow a foot.

I offer my hand to him and smile at his resemblance to Blaydon. "How you doing?" I ask, patting his shoulder.

He shrugs and nods his head, then looks over to Jasper and holds up a game. "Jasp, the new one, you up for some Xbox?"

Jasper lowers Mikey to the floor and clasps his hand. "Sure we are, silly question, little man."

Jase scoffs and jabs him in the stomach as he walks past him. "Less of the little, I'm nearly taller than you."

I roll my eyes and nod a greeting to Sammy who chuckles as he watches the squabble ensue with Jasp, now holding Jase in a head lock and Mikey pulling on both their trouser legs.

I pull my cell from my pocket when I feel it vibrating, and gesture to Sammy that I'm taking a call. I move towards the pool house. "Jefferson."

"Hey, Derek. It's Maggie. I have the results to those DNA tests you wanted put through. Do you want me to tell you now, or shall I leave the mail on your desk?"

"No, tell me."

I end the call and release the breath I was holding. River comes into view, followed by the vision that is Kyra, her red silky locks hiding her face from my view, and I take a few minutes to compose myself. I hadn't realised how much I actually cared either way about the results. To me, Mikey is Sammy and River's son regardless of the DNA that runs in his makeup. River was being irrational about the Danny business; she was proof that just because someone's parent was dark and evil it doesn't define who their children will become. It was the fact that Danny could take such a claim, such a great thing that came out of this that burned and stoked the fire of hate that always burned inside my gut for him.

I make my way towards them, each step matching the heavy thump in my chest.

"I'm fine, Sammy. I just needed water."

"I can't believe you didn't call me. What if something bad *did* happen? And where was Mikey? He was with you when I left the studio this morning and yet was here when I arrived."

"I went and got him from the hospital," I say, and cringe when Sammy's hard stare turns to me. Not many men can effect or intimidate me, but where River was concerned, Sammy was an alpha male king of the jungle not to be fucked with.

"You fucking knew about this and didn't call me?"

"I didn't know until later and by then she was fine and being released, so no point in phoning and worrying you while you were driving." I watch him digest what I've told him and the logic behind it. "Listen guys, about the DNA."

"No!" River shakes her head and rests her hand on my chest. "I don't want to get the test done. Mikey is our boy, mine and Sammy's, and nothing can change that."

Sammy looks to me with a furrowed brow and then to River, confused by her change of heart. "Nothing can change that, Riv."

She smiles. "I know. So I don't need to get the test."

I rest my hand on her shoulder and gently grasp the nape of her neck. "I already ran the tests, sweetheart." I chance a quick look to Sammy; his breathing has increased and I see pain flash in his eyes. "He's your son." I refocus my gaze on her. Her green orbs have filled with unshed tears and her bottom lip quivers.

"What?" she whispers, faintly.

"Confirmed. Sammy is his father, Riv."

A strangled, choking sound comes from Sammy and he drops to his knees.

Jasper

When I met Sammy in college, he was broken, heartbroken. We bonded over some frat girl who was sticking her tongue down my throat all night at a college bar. When I went outside to take a call, I came back to find her on her knees in a corner booth with Sammy throat deep in her. I bought him a beer, took a seat, and waited my turn. I didn't even have to ask her, she just finished Sammy off and moved on to me. Turned out her boyfriend had cheated on her and she was rebelling to teach him a lesson. He tried to teach me one when he caught her under our table with my dick in her hand. Sammy had my back and I had his from that day on. We're like brothers, and hearing Derek tell him Mikey is, in fact, his washed relief through me like never before.

  Watching him fall to his knees and sob nearly made me come undone. River pulls from Der and throws herself at Sammy, climbing into his lap and they cry together. I sense the ache, the joy and love for them that I feel reflected in Derek. I grab him into a hug; this is huge for our family. River needed the peace of mind and Sammy had a right to know, no matter how he felt either way.

"I'm so fucking happy for them," I breathe into his ear.

His arms come around my back and squeeze. "Me too."

I pull away and reach for River, pulling her into me. Sammy gets to his feet, swipes his face and grins. "Time to celebrate. Apart from his birth, this is the happiest day of my life. I knew he was mine, but fuck, this feels good. Where is he? Go get our son out here, Twink, he needs to know this too."

We share a chuckle and move inside to get drinks. Kyra's beautiful cheeks are flushed, her eyes glistening from the tears. We all felt the power from the relief for Sammy and River; she hadn't been a part of our lives long, but she was quickly becoming a member of our family.

The evening wore on, and after food, we all came inside to give Jase his gifts. I kept sensing River's and Derek's eyes on me, and was beginning to get paranoid that they were planning something. I was on guard whenever Der came near me, but neither said anything to me and I was relieved. With Hannah still away, all this shit with Mikey aired out, I was feeling fucking happy for once. All my favourite people were in the same room and there was birthday cake.

Kyra

The atmosphere has been tense; the way Jasper stiffens whenever Derek goes near him is odd. He hasn't been acting like his usual fun-loving, anything-goes self. His blue eyes sparkle whenever they fall upon me and my heart stops, then re-beats as soon as he turns his gaze from mine.

I release the breath I was holding and go back to the kitchen where River and Derek are clearing plates, but my footing falters when I hear the muffled conversation they're having. I hold my breath and debate going back to Sammy and Jasper, but it's too late. The internal battle lasts too long and the knowledge I hear cannot be unheard.

"I've always known you feel for him, Derek. I just know Jasp isn't like that, but I have seen subtle changes, looks traded, and the shift in atmosphere."

"You've always known?"

"Of course I know."

"And you don't care that I like men as well as women?"

"I love you, and I'll love whoever you choose to spend your life with—male or female. Why would you ever question that?"

"Nothing is happening with Jasper. He doesn't know how I feel, never has and doesn't need to know."

"Are you sure about that? Because he's acting different around you."

"I think he's just feeling weird about this whole Hannah situation."

I *had* sensed something; I know the way Derek looks at Jasp is with deep emotion, but hearing it confirmed leaves me light-headed.

I tiptoe back into where the guys are packing away Jase's birthday gifts. He's staying at River and Sammy's tonight, and I'm spending the night here, but I need a drink; I need to settle the buzzing in my mind. I pour myself a glass and gulp it down.

River emerges from the kitchen and hugs Jasp. "Thank you for getting all this ready today." He kisses her cheek and pats her bottom while looking smug at Sammy, who just rolls his eyes.

"Let me help you load the car with your stuff," Derek tells Jase, walking into the room and taking it from Jase's hands.

Sammy scoops a sleeping Mikey up and follows Derek out to the car.

"It was nice to see you again, Kyra. Call me sometime." Jase winks at me. I smile, but feel the creep of a blush. "Hey playboy, you need to grow a few inches before you can play in that pond," Jasp jests, throwing a cushion at him.

"I'm almost as tall as you!"

"Keep dreaming!" He grabs him in a head lock, dragging him from the room with him struggling and landing blows to Jasper's stomach.

I refill my glass and begin pottering to keep my thoughts from rendering me incapable of being in their presence. I turn the TV off and put away the controllers for the Xbox.

"Hey, I can do that." I startle at Jasper's voice and giggle. Crap, the wine is making me giddy. His face beams down at me, his perfect teeth on display. I go sit at the table, pouring more wine. Derek comes to join me and Jasper follows suit.

Jasper

"So, tell me about this ex-boyfriend of yours. Der knows, but I'm curious, did you end on bad terms?" I want to know why she would think he would send her a note or be stalking her. Der was vague when sharing details. I watch her eyes dart between Derek and me before she answers.

"My mom and dad are church going folk. They believe I should marry before enjoying the… fruits of life, so to speak." Her cheeks redden; she's so fucking cute.

"So to speak? You mean… before having sex?" I know what she meant, but watching her bite that plump bottom lip and shift in her seat has to be done.

She nods her head. "My high school boyfriend didn't think the same way. He said we would be getting married, so he didn't see why we shouldn't be doing it. The sex." She gestures towards me and I can't help the grin that breaks across my face. She tugs a loose strand of hair behind her ear and looks to Derek; he smiles at her, the warmth in his eyes telling me he has feelings for her. I can't decipher what I feel about that. His eyes turn to me and my head automatically nods. *Yes, she is something special.*

"I'm not a prude or anything, but I just had a… sixth sense if you like, about him. I stayed with him for my parents. They were friends with his and we grew up together, but he changed a lot and I didn't really feel *that* way about him. He sought sexual satisfaction from a friend of mine, giving me the excuse I needed to end things." She shrugs her shoulders and sips the wine Derek poured for her. "He didn't take it well and bombarded me with letters; love letters that then became hostile. He turned my friends against me and living there was unbearable in the end, so I moved." She downs the remains of her wine and holds her glass out to Derek to refill.

My fists clench. "Hostile?"

She shrugs again. "He got a bit hands-on one night, cornering me when I was coming from the studio I trained at. That was the final straw for me. My mom and dad wanted me to stay, but I always planned to leave, anyway. I heard he married said friend he cheated on me with, but they spilt. She was having an affair with his friend. Karma." She grins and I have to bite my lips. Fuck, she's gorgeous.

"So you think it was him who sent the note?"

She taps her glass with her finger, "He sent them before, I just assumed…"

"What about after him? Other boyfriends?"

She chokes on the wine she just tipped into her mouth. Derek leans over to pat her back. "Thank you," she splutters. I hand her a napkin and smile. "I haven't really dated anyone else." She manages to answer without making eye contact. God, I knew she was innocent, but not that innocent. I change the subject to something lighter and watch her blossom; the wine has taken over and makes her giggle every time Derek or I say anything slightly amusing. I watch Derek watch her and I can't sort through the feelings I'm having. It's want mixed with contentment being with them.

"I need to use the ladies room," Kyra announces in a fake, poor English accent. Her footing is unsteady. Derek jumps up to steady her, guiding her to the bathroom; I hear her giggling to him, saying she drank too much. I move some of the cushions as she stumbles back in, closely followed by Derek. I pat the seat and hold my hands out to her. She smiles, making me inhale sharply. I want her so fucking bad. "You're so beautiful," she murmurs, reaching out to stroke my cheek.

"You're drunk," I tell her, helping her lie back on the couch.

"So lovely, Jasper. No wonder Derek wants you, who wouldn't?"

My brow furrows at her drunken talk. The hairs rise on my neck, and Derek has become completely still, his posture rigid. "You're drunk, Ky," I reiterate.

She exhales, then yawns. "Drunk or not, it's the truth." Her eyes close.

Derek makes a hasty exit, leaving me bewildered. I pull a blanket over her, grab the glasses, and take them through to the kitchen.

Derek leans with his palms flat against the sideboard, his shoulders tense. His head is bowed down toward the floor and he's muttering cuss words.

"She's out for the night," I tell him, making him tense at the sound of my voice. I place the glasses in the sink and turn to find Derek's smouldering gaze on me. He has a way of making me feel stripped bare with just a look. I had always been in control, the dominant participant in my sexual adventures, but Derek has me squirming in my fucking skin. I've lived with him for six years and never thought about him in any way other than as my good friend, so what has changed?

What's happening to me? What is he doing?

"What was Kyra talking about in there, Derek?" I ask in an accusing tone.

He straightens to his full height, his fist clenching, and the tic in his jaw prominent. He takes a couple of steps in my direction. "I'm bisexual." His voice is laced with a heightened energy. His eyes pin and hold me captive in their impenetrable gaze. "And I want to fuck you."

He continues towards me. My mouth feels sealed shut, my mind tries to process what he just said, but the blood rushes to my cock, confusing and scaring the shit out of me. He's too close; I'm not bisexual, so why am I shaking? His breath wisps across my face, making me inhale sharply and swallow the rush of saliva filling my mouth. His body brushes against mine gently like a whisper of a promise. His head lowers, his lips next to my ear. I feel like I'm vibrating from the nerves and the electric energy filling the room.

"And you want me to fuck you too, Jasper. I can see it, feel it." His face turns, his full lips brushing against mine. I'm frozen, my mind at war with what my body is telling me."Mmm, I can taste it." He moves his head back and studies my face for what feels like a lifetime before the heat emanating from him leaves me and I'm standing alone in the kitchen, completely stunned.

* * * * *

Derek carries Kyra up to River's old reading room and places her in bed. When he steps out, his eyes hold mine for a few heart stomping seconds before he goes to his room, closing the door and leaving me left to toss and turn all night. He was right when he said I wanted him too. I can't explain it because I don't understand what's happening to me, but knowing Kyra is mere feet away and across the hall, and Derek is in his room thinking about me, wanting me… fuck! It's left my blood on boil. Everything is changing; why now? This can't be happening. I'm just going through a meltdown over the new shit in my life. This is all just about Hannah and the baby, that's all this is. It all comes back to that. That's all this is, that's all this is.

* * * * *

I shower and dress quickly, and leave without grabbing the usual coffee with Derek. I can't deal with it right now. I was up all night trying to understand what changed in me, what's different. I want a man; I am really fucking craving him.

I drive to the office and work over the documentation Sammy wants to discuss. I lose myself in the work and it's a relief not to be consumed by Derek for a little while.

"Hey, man. What time did you get here?" Sammy asks, entering the office.

"Not long ago. I wanted an early start. I have a lunch date with River today." I grin at him, and he points his finger at me and raises an eyebrow.

"I wouldn't be smug; she's on some weird River-save-Jasper mission. She keeps telling me you're not right and you're struggling with all this shit."

I roll my eyes and slap the folder on the table. "It's all new. It's just going to take time to get used to it all, and it doesn't help that Hannah is looking at it like a fucking business agreement. I feel sorry for our fucking kid. This is a clusterfuck. I haven't even told my dad yet. You know what he's like about family and meeting the one and shit." I swipe my hands through my hair and lean back, letting the chair tilt and take my weight.

"Listen it's not the best way things could have gone and I really want you to settle down, Jasp, but you're doing this all for the wrong reasons."

"Sammy, they're the only reasons. You know how I feel about this stuff. I never wanted kids or marriage, but life sometimes throws you a curve ball and you just have to adjust to it. You of all people know what it's like growing up with a shitty parent. I won't risk her meeting some prick and letting him raise my kid, no fucking way." Hannah is due back tomorrow. She told me she's staying with her parents for the night and wants to meet for breakfast in the morning to discuss things.

"Hey." My insides stir at the sound of Derek's voice. I don't know where to look. I know I can't look at him. Sammy would see it all over my face, so I lift some files and will my eyes to stare at them.

"Hey," I manage to get past my dry throat.

Sammy greets him with a handshake. "What are you doing here?" Sammy asks, taking a seat on the corner of the desk.

"I wanted to let you know in person that we're pretty sure we have this guy connected with the stalker cases."

I lower the files to find his gaze on me. I shift and briefly flick my eyes to Sammy. He stands and grabs Derek in a hug. "That's great fucking news." Derek returns his hug with a hard pat on Sammy's shoulder.

"Where's Kyra?" I ask.

He fucking smirks at me. "She's on our couch after losing her stomach contents down the john. She feels like shit and can't remember anything she did or said since River and

Sammy left."

Sammy folds his arms and grins at Derek. "What did she do or say?"

Derek's eyes slowly drag themselves from me and return Sammy's grin. "Just the usual drunken garble people say when they're intoxicated."

Sammy looks to me and then back to Derek. "You know what they say; truth comes out when you're drunk. Did she declare love?"

"She declared Jasp is beautiful," Derek informs him, making him burst into a fit of laughter.

"Fuck, you are, too." He leans over and pinches my cheeks. "Like a little princess."

I bat his hand from my cheek. "Prick." I stand, jumping out of the way of Sammy's fist coming towards my upper arm. "I'm out," I laugh, brushing past Derek to get to the door. His scent invades my senses, sending the message to my dick that it's him.

"Where you going?" Sammy calls out.

I stroke a hand down my face. "I have a date with your wife. She's like Ky, can't get enough of this beautiful face." I wink and dodge the pen he throws at me from the desk.

"What about the file I wanted?" he shouts.

"On the desk, asshole," I shout back, pushing the door to exit.

I don't have to meet River until this afternoon, but my mind and dick are still having communicational problems, and the last thing I need is Sammy picking up on the weird shit going on with Derek and me. My life is complicated enough and I just need to let this shit, whatever it is, pass.

"Jasp."

I stop dead and take a few calming breaths before I turn

to face Derek, who like a sneaky fucking ninja, has followed me out.

"What's up?" I ask, over-gesturing a chin lift like we're fucking homies. I clear my throat, slipping my hands into my pocket to stop myself from picking the eyelash from his cheek.

"I wanted to ask if you'll check in on Kyra, take her some food. I have some paperwork and things to do and won't be home until tonight. Sammy just said he'll pick her up on his way home and take her back there until we figure out about finding her a new place."

"Why can't she go home if you've found this guy? Who is he, anyway?" I had a million questions for him when he walked in and said they had this guy, but I couldn't be around him in front of Sammy, not in such a small space.

"He crashed his car, one we were looking for in connection with this case, and there was evidence inside to support the theory."

"He crashed his car?"

"Yes, Jasper. I shouldn't be sharing this with you. He's in the ICU and we're not sure if he'll make it."

Karma; she works in her own unique way.

I shift from foot to foot. "So why can't she go home?"

"Because I don't want her in that shitty apartment. It's not secure enough or nice enough for her, don't you agree?" The way he looks at me is like he wants an answer to a question he hasn't actually asked. His eyes are on fire with so much emotion I nearly combust under their intensity.

"No, you're right. That place is a shit hole."

He nods, looking away and releasing me from the hold his eyes locked me in. Fuck, how long can we keep this up?

He turns from me and walks to his car, calling over his shoulder, "Take Beauty some food, Jasp."

Kyra

My head has a marching band inside it, which is the only explanation I can come up with for the pounding inside my brain.

"Argh!" I groan, rolling onto my back. My eyes spring open as the images from last night filter in. *Oh crap. I said stuff to Jasper about Derek.* I roll back onto my front, bite the pillow, and bash my fists down while mumbling into the fabric.

"Stupid, stupid stuu…ARGHHH!" I nearly vomit from the scare of someone laughing in the room. I spin round to find Derek chuckling beside me.

"Hey. I was sitting at the window, waiting for you to wake up."

If a pothole would open up under this bed right now and pull me into it, I would be grateful. This morning already sucked and I knew my skin matched the colour of my hair.

"How'd you sleep?"

Oh, God. I could kiss him for ignoring my outburst.

"Fi… hurmmm, fine thank you," I mumble.

"Red really suits you, Beauty." He smiles.

I stroke a strand of my hair. "It's my natural colour."

He grins and reaches across to stroke my heated cheek. "Oh, I know, and it's gorgeous."

I turn an even brighter red. I can feel it, and would probably be glowing if it was night time.

"How do you feel?" he asks, still stroking my cheek. I move into his touch like a cat would when caressed. He makes me feel so safe and protected. His comfort is just that: a rare comfort.

"Mmmm, better now," I coo and he chuckles. It's a stunning sound.

"You want to come eat?" My stomach rejects the idea as soon as it leaves his mouth. I dart from the bed to the bathroom; trying to be sick and kick the door shut is no easy task.

* * * * *

I come down stairs after emptying my stomach lining down the toilet, and showering the dew from my skin.

"Hey, I made you fresh orange and left two aspirin on the table. Go lay in front of the TV. I'll be back to check on you later today." He kisses my cheek.

I reach for him as he tries to leave. "Derek, wait."

He sucks his bottom lip into his mouth and turns to me, his face seeming hard, his eyes accusing. He lifts his brows and nods his head in a silent command for me to speak.

I feel nervous and hesitant, my stomach fluttering, the tension making my muscle stiffen from his hostile stance. "I just wanted to say sorry for getting that way and being an ass."

His posture relaxes, and he lets out a breath. "You're not an ass, Beauty, and nothing you said wasn't true."

My eyes widen at his statement. He watches me, waiting for my reaction. Acceptance, maybe. I reach onto my tiptoe and lay a kiss on his lips. I smile when his eyes melt like caramel chocolate. "I see why, and anyone would be lucky to have you want them," I whisper.

He grips my back to prevent me from moving away, his lips press hard on mine, stamping himself on me, marking me, owning me. He pulls away, our breathing heavy, raising our chests in a flurry of erratic breaths.

"Then consider yourself really, really lucky, Beauty." He moves past me, leaving me unsteady on my feet. *Wow.*

* * * * *

Stupid movie gets me every time. I sniffle, wiping my eyes.

"Ky! Where are you?" Jasper calls, coming through the lobby. I rub at my eyes and nose to catch any dampness and click the TV off.

"Argh, there you are." He walks towards me, his dark hair styled neatly for once. He ring faded jeans that sit low on his hips; his shirt is dark like his hair. God, why is he so beautiful? *Beautiful.* Oh God, I said that to him last night.

He drops a bag on the floor, his face losing all its enthusiasm and usual cocky smirk. He drops to his knees in front of me; my heart skips in my chest like a skipping stone on a lake before sinking. His hands reach up, the pads of his thumbs swiping under my eyes. "What happened?" he asks, his minty breath washing over me. He's so close, I can taste his breath. He moves even closer and my heart seizes in my chest.

"Ky, please talk to me, baby. What's wrong? Why were you crying?"

Coherent thoughts return in haste. I shake my head and move back so our lips aren't inches apart and too unbelievably tempting. "I was watching a film." I squirm in my seat and look away from the gentle pull of his eyes. "The Notebook." I cough, bite my lip, and look anywhere but at him. I feel the sofa vibrating slightly and realize it's him laughing. I pick up a cushion and swat him with it; he laughs harder and snatches it from me, lifting it and bringing it down across my thigh. I screech and fall into a bout of giggles.

"The fucking Notebook. I thought someone had died!" He strains to get the words out through his laughter.

I sit up straight and try to be serious. "Someone did die and it was freaking sad!"

He launches himself at me, his hands tickling the sensitive skin on my stomach. I can hardly breathe from his relentless tickling. I feel his weight grow heavier over my frame as I shift and he slips between my thighs. I gasp. He has become completely still over me. I risk looking up at him, and the blue in his eyes looks like it's swirling like the current at sea, raging from an incredible pull just below the surface.

I can't hide the effect he has on me, and my body betrays me, flooding me in arousal between my thighs. My nipples harden and peak through my tank top as his eyes roam mine, then ignite a path down my jaw, the valley of my chest, over my breasts, down my navel, and rest where his crotch is mere centimetres from mine.

"Jasper."

My body wants him so badly to grind against me, give me some desperate relief from the ache that's building. But the fact he's taken, and Derek and I are kind of trying, maybe working towards something, and the fact that Derek wants Jasper too makes me pause.

The front door opens and closes, then the sound of clicking heels echoing up the lobby makes both our eyes snap to each other. Jasper's grow wide; he scurries to get off me, straightening his shirt. I sit up just as River walks in. She eyes us suspiciously, and points her finger at me. I feel like a teenager under the strict eye of my mother when she caught me doing wrong.

"Have you been watching those sad movies again?"

I sigh, every muscle in my body relaxing. I hadn't even noticed I had completely tensed up.

"Yep, she has. She was a blubbering mess." Jasper grins, pleased with himself.

"I don't know why you're acting the big I am." River points to him. "You cried over Marley and Me."

His face drops, his mouth popping open. "That was a dog, it was totally different and you promised! That's it, no more movie nights with you." He pouts.

She rolls her eyes and points down to his jeans. "Stop being dramatic or I'll tell everyone I came in here to find Kyra crying and you sporting an erection."

She lifts an eyebrow and I rethink the wanting a hole to swallow me this morning; if it could come right now and swallow me whole that would be great. I don't know who to look at or what to say, but Jasper prevents me from doing anything. I flash my eyes to him to find his usual sexy smirk firmly in place.

"And I'll just tell your husband you were checking out my package."

"That wouldn't be the first time he's heard that pass your lips. Now come on, I'm eating for two here." She gestures to her stomach. "Come on, Mommy's hungry." She smiles and waves over her shoulder at me.

I'm grateful the studio is closed today because the thought of moving anywhere makes my stomach curdle. Jasper grabs the bag he dropped when he walked in and brings it to me. "I got you some bottled water and a sub sandwich for when you're feeling up to it."

I take the bag from him and watch his ass as he leaves.

Derek

I'm sick of fighting this. Sick of watching, aching, wanting. It was bearable before because I had convinced myself it could never happen. Jasp would never be interested, but the fucking way he looks at me, I know he does and I've denied myself for too long. Kyra and I could have something. She's the perfect girl, and any guy would want her. I *do* want her and will have her. I just need to sate my yearning for Jasper first. I just need to know what it would be like to have him under me, in me. God, I'm hornier than a frat boy.

"Here's the picture, it's the best we could do with the tubes in." I take the photo of the suspect and drive to Caroline's, the secretary and fourth victim of this asshole; she had taken some time off work, but recovered well.

She opens the door; she must have seen me pull up. She's in casual attire which is something I've never seen her in. Her jeans seem a little loose on her smaller frame.

"You've lost weight, Caroline," I say, and she shrugs.

"I'm just coping with everything. Give me time, I'll be fine. Drink?" she asks, gesturing for me to take a seat.

"No thanks, I brought the photo I told you about."

"I told you Derek I didn't see his face." She wrings her hands together in front of her.

"I know, sweetheart. Come sit down." She breathes out a rush of air and takes the seat next to me. "Listen." I take her hands in mine. "Sometimes we don't even realise we may have seen things. Maybe he came into the office, or you saw him in the parking lot before it happened. I want to make sure I have the right guy here to keep other women safe."

A tear leaks to her cheek she swipes it. "I'm sorry, I'm being silly. Okay, show me."

I pat her knee, leaning in to look in her now downcast eyes. "You're allowed to feel the way you do, Caroline. You were a victim of a vicious crime. You can be sad, silly, and reluctant. You have a right to feel." She lifts her eyes and nods her head. I pull the picture from the file and hand it to her.

I watch her study the image. "I'm sorry. I don't recognise him." I smile to reassure her it's okay. "Is he going to die?" she mutters.

"We don't know yet. He is in pretty bad shape, though, and all the evidence points to him at this juncture."

"Thank you. It will make leaving the house easier knowing you found him."

"You ever have a bad day when you're worried about leaving the house alone, you call me, do you understand?" I reach under her chin and bring her face to mine. Seeing the tears wash across her eyes, the fear in them brings me back to the day I saw it in Mya's, and my chest tightens. The pang of grief that lives in my heart spreads like a an open wound, staining my insides and coating my emotions in a heavy fog.

"Call me, okay?" I stand, leaving her, and go back to the car to call River.

"Hey, baby. What's up?" She sounds happy and it's so

good to hear that in her voice. "Der, what's wrong?" I hear Jasper in the background asking her what's wrong, then a shuffling noise down the line. "Hey, I've come outside, talk to me," she says.

"I just had a moment. I miss her, you know."

Her breathing blows through the line. "I know, Der. Go speak to her. Tell her how you're feeling."

* * * * *

I take the painful drive to where Mya ended her life; the winding roads tormenting me with every bend, the trees mocking me as I pass them, and my soul fading the closer I get. It's hard on my sanity coming here, the painful ache growing, spreading throughout me like a cancer , but sometimes it's the only place I feel close to her and can remember her clearly. The memories are becoming like an apparition of her. I just want to see her clearly and tell her I love her.

Time does help you heal, but it doesn't fade the love you feel, and with love comes the ache and loneliness when you allow the grief to overcome you.

I pull the car up and step out, the ghost of my past self coming here that night assaults me as the despair renders me incapable of moving.

I slump back against the car, slide to the ground and just sit.

Jasper

"Was that Derek? Is he okay?" I ask River as she walks back into the restaurant. I recognise the pain in her eyes. She's thinking of Blay, which means Derek is having a bad day. They don't happen often, maybe a few times a year, but it hits him hard.

My heart fucking hurts right now for them. "Is he at the cliff top?" I had followed him there before under the orders of River, to just sit in the car and wait him out.

"Yeah, go."

I kiss her cheek. "Are you sure you're okay with me leaving you? Want me to ring Sammy?"

"No, no, go. I'll ring him and let him know I'm getting Kyra. Go get Derek, Jasp. Take him home."

"Okay." I kiss her again, then make my way to Derek.

It takes me over an hour to get to him. I find him sitting propped against his car; he doesn't even flinch when I pull up, neither does he look in my direction.

I walk to him and slide down next to him. "She's not here, Der."

He turns to face me; the red straining the whites of his

eyes tightens my chest.

"Don't take my only comfort away, Jasp. She's here."

I rest my hand over his heart. "This is where she is. Always. You don't need to come here to talk to her. She's always with you, she can hear you from wherever you are. Let's go home and get a drink. Ky's gone home with River."

He looks down at my hand, then out into the horizon. The sun is a golden orb shining back at him, kissing his skin and lighting his face. He has a chiselled jaw that tics when he's concentrating on something, or is upset. His nose is a perfect shape. His lips are full; dark lashes blanket his eyes. I can feel the muscles flex in his pec where my hand lays.

"Jasp! I said, okay."

"I'm sorry, what?" I ask him. I had completely zoned out.

"I said okay, let's go. I'll follow you."

I pull my hand from his chest and jump to my feet. "Okay."

* * * * *

I pour him his third scotch. He hasn't said a word since we came in and I don't want to push him. *Food. I'll go with food.*

"You hungry?"

He shakes his head and holds his glass up for another shot. *Fuck, think... River.*

"So, River seemed great today. She had colour in her cheeks, laughed and joked."

His eyes rise to find mine and I inhale harshly at the pain in his gaze. "I have days where I feel like I failed her and I miss her so fucking bad it takes every ounce of strength not to throw myself off to join her."

I feel sick.

"It's not all the time just… I have bad days. I thought this guy doing these crimes was her ex. But it wasn't like Danny, that bastard still haunts me …it's not just the dead that haunt people, the living can, too." He shoots back the scotch. "I was convinced it must be him and then"—he rubs his hand across his forehead—"it wasn't, it's just some fuck. He had a couple priors for possession, lived in a shit hole on the other side of town, no family."

I walk around the bar. "That's a good thing, right?"

He stands and walks over to the fireplace; he skims some of the photos with his fingertips. "I wanted to finally fucking have Evan in my grasp, feel his pulse dim under my hand. I didn't want to be responsible for what happened to these women, but it was something I was willing to be if it meant getting to end that bastard. Why didn't she come to me? Let me look after her? Mend her?"

His voice breaks and so do my insides. I had never felt so heartbroken and in need to comfort in my whole life. He was hurting and my heart hurt for him, above everything, he was my good friend and I felt his suffering. I go and stand behind him, resting my palm on his shoulder. "Why don't you have pictures of her?" I had noticed this in the years living with him, but had never asked why there were none.

"My mom blames me, and she wouldn't let me have any. I don't have anything of hers, just a fading fucking image in my head." His voice wavers as the emotions mix with alcohol.

I guide him to the couch and he slumps into the seat. "You should eat something. Should I order?" I ask, watching him rest his head back and close his eyes.

"Just sit with me, Jasp. Just give me that."

I sit next to him, bewildered by his simple request. Why would he say it like I might refuse? My mind shuts up when my dick twitches. He lays his head in my lap; I rest my arms over the back of the sofa and don't even breathe. The back of his head rests on my thigh, too fucking close to my growing dick. He shifts, kicking his legs over the arm of the sofa, so he's lying across the couch. I watch his eyes flutter closed. I can't move and if I'm being honest with myself, I don't want to. I want to give him this comfort. I want to ease his pain somehow and if just sitting here like this is a way to do that, then I will. I'll sit here all night.

* * * * *

I shift and an ache twinges my neck. "Argh, fuck," I moan, reaching up and rubbing the knot out. I feel the weight shift in my lap and freeze. I must have fallen asleep and Derek has still got his head in my lap, right over my dick. *Think about something else, think about something else. Derek's face is on your crotch! Fuck, think about something else. Sammy; okay, yeah that works. River and Michael, okay let's keep going. Jase, Kyra… fuck Kyra, Kyra and me, mmmm Kyra and Derek, fuck Derek and me ….and Kyra.*

"I'll make coffee." Derek's gravelly voice bursts my thoughts as he jumps from the sofa like it's caught fire. I look down at the huge erection I'm sporting; I guess my cock poking him in the ear took him by surprise. The couch fucking did catch fire.

I make my way to my room to shower and change. Checking my cell, I notice several missed calls from Hannah. I hit her number and listen for the few rings before she answers.

"Jasper, God where were you? I called last night."

I try to shake off the dread she instils in me. "I'm sorry Han, I got caught up with something. What's up?"

"Mom has a few dresses she likes here, and as long as we

do the wedding in the next couple months, the alterations can be made."

I fight back the retort my mind is desperate to give her and steady my voice. "Okay, well if you like them, what do you need from me?"

I hear a male in the background say her name and then the line goes silent. "Hannah, who was that?"

There's silence for a few seconds before she speaks again. "Sorry, room service. I needed some ginger for the sickness."

"The room service guy knows you by name?" I ask, not really giving a shit, it's just bizarre.

"Well, I get morning sickness, so he comes here daily, Jasper. What are you trying to imply?"

I didn't need this shit. "Nothing, I only asked a question. Fuck, Hannah."

"Do you have to say that WORD?" she screeches, and I move the phone from my ear until she stops her little rant.

"Hannah! What do you need from me for this? Money?"

"No, Mom's paying. I just wanted to let you know that it'll take an extra couple of days if we go ahead to buy. Mom wants to be one hundred percent, so she wants to check out a couple of different boutiques. She's set up appointments for the next couple days."

I have no clue why she would need an appointment to shop, or why it took her going away for over a week to pick a wedding dress. This is why I love River; she's like a guy where that stuff is concerned. One shop, go in, get what you need and get out.

"That's fine, just make sure you like whatever she picks, Hannah. This is your wedding." I couldn't put any enthusiasm into the word wedding; it was a foreign word to me, and something I never planned on having. *Shit, I really need to call my dad.*

* * * * *

The next few days are the same at home; a tense atmosphere when Derek and I are together, and me trying to avoid him. I eat my meals out, come in late, work out, and go to bed, but my body has some fucked up connection to his and just knowing he's in the house, bedroom, shower… Fuck I'm losing it, and masturbating like a high school kid on Viagra.

Kyra has been busy learning all the manager crap at Twinkle Toes, so I haven't seen her and I'm nervous about having them all round for family night.

River is like a physic when it comes to us; she knows everything a lot of the time before we even know we're feeling it.

I stop at a convenience store a few blocks away on my way home from work. I buy milk, and treats for Mikey, and slowly make my way back to the car. This chore has taken me all of twenty minutes, nowhere near long enough to keep my inner battles about Derek from driving me in-fucking-sane. But I can't stay out forever. People are expecting me, and I need to man the fuck up.

I open the door and slip into my car. I'm about to pull out when I see Hannah's mom chatting to a women outside a hair salon. *What the fuck?* I pull out my cell and text Hannah.

You didn't tell me you were coming back today.

Two minutes later I receive a reply.

I'm not, I'll be back in a few days. H

I stare over at her mother. It's her without a doubt; I would know that stiff upper lip anywhere.

Did you and your mom decide on a dress?

No, she wants to be sure, so we're going back to the first ones again. H

Why is she lying to me? I step from the car, hold my phone up, snap a picture of her mom and send it to her. I wait for a reply for thirty minutes.

Asshole!!

Yeah, I'm the asshole. She's lying to me.

You better not be fucking someone else with my baby in your stomach, Hannah!

The phone rings in my hand, startling me, making me nearly drop it.
"What's your problem, Jasper? Why do you have to be so crude and rude? And if I were, I wouldn't be doing anything different than you are." Her irate voice screeches at me down the line.
"You told me you're with your mother, and yet I'm staring at her, Hannah. And I'm not fucking anyone."
She breathes heavy down the line. "Well, you should get that out your system now, Jasper. Because once we're married and the baby comes, there will be none of that."
Is she for real? "You're telling the man you're going to

marry to go fuck around?"

"I'm not naïve, Jasper. I know who you are, and let's not act like this is love."

She's right, it's not and I am who I am. I fuck a lot of women, so why does her saying it twist my gut? "Why am I looking at your mother, Hannah?"

"Fine! I'm a little freaked out by everything and just needed a break, okay? My mother already has the dress. It's disgusting and already a size smaller because she likes to rub it in that I'm not a skinny bride like she was."

Why she didn't just tell me all this? Like I would begrudge her time away. Her mom is spiteful; who would want to make their kid feel like shit? The dress, she already had it, and I probably won't even notice when I'm having a panic attack at the altar.

"Why do you let her make you feel that way? And why didn't you just tell me this shit?"

"Because. Now are you okay with me being gone a little longer?"

"Yeah, take as long as you need. Just make sure you're looking after yourself and our baby." She's silent for a few beats before saying goodbye and hanging up.

I hadn't really thought about what a big change this is for her. She always seemed to just be okay with it and treat me like a sign-on-the-dotted-line business associate. I put my cell away and drive home.

I really love this place, and I'll miss the luxury, familiarity, and home comfort it offers when I finally have to move out.

Sammy's car is parked up front, so I have no more time to hide my internal conflict; I need to put on my game face.

I push the door open and hear Mikey's laughter. I drop my keys in the bowl on the console table and follow the sound.

I round the corner and nearly collide with Kyra. She smiles, then bites her lip; my eyes watch intently at her subtle innocent reaction to me and straight away my brain fires off positions I want her in.

"I'm playing hide and go seek with Mikey," she says. I hear a giggle and look over at the Mikey-shaped bulge in the curtain.

I shake my head and hold my hand over my mouth, leaning down to whisper in Kyra's ear. "He'll stay there all day if he thinks you haven't found him. Kid free afternoon?"

She gapes at me and slaps my arm. I feel a slap around my head and know Sammy has heard me. "You're a mean uncle. You can do that with your own kid. Mine has an out of control mother who wants him to wash up and get ready to eat." Mikey's giggle attracts Sammy's attention and gives me a second to look over Kyra's outfit, another summer dress stopping above her knee, displaying those toned beauties for my viewing pleasure. It's red today; she seems to coordinate her wardrobe with her eyes and hair. I chance a look at the sliver of cleavage showing and feel another slap around the head.

"River's in there waiting for us. Stop eye fucking Kyra and move it!" he whisper shouts at me. I look around to make sure Mikey didn't hear him, but he's bolted. Kyra's eyes widen, the green orbs big. She's stunned by Sammy's comment.

"Fine, a twofer suits me." I grin at his scowl.

"What's a twofer?" Kyra asks, and Sammy raises his brow at me, then leans around me to answer her.

"Oh, he just means he gets to eye fuck you both, rather than just you."

I hear her little gasp and I chuckle. They know I don't see River that way. I'm a man and can still appreciate her beauty, just more in a brother kind of way.

"Hey, baby, there you are." River grips me in a hug and squeezes.

I feel him. I can feel his eyes on me, searing into my skin. When she releases me, my eyes hit his. How can he make me feel this way? It's just Derek, I berate myself.

I can't hold any of the conversations at the table. I can't taste the little bit of food I've forced down my throat. I know his eyes are on me. I can't concentrate on River and Kyra telling me how well Ky is doing and how quickly she picked up the business side of things at Twinkle Toes. I can't focus on the details because Derek has ensnared me in this fucked up game he's playing.

I can't eat. I can't sleep. I can't work. Derek has infected my brain. Every thought is of him and how he's fucking with my head, my body.

Does wanting him make me gay? I look over at Sammy; he's a really good looking guy. Women love him, but I feel only brotherly love for him, no sexual tension, no fucking ache in my stomach telling me having him is a necessity. It's just Derek.

Kyra comes into view; her beautiful face holds such purity. Her laugh, so light and airy, breaks into my inner thoughts. She's free, a free soul. If I was gay, I wouldn't be getting hard right now just watching her. I wish I was more than the guy just looking for a good time, then maybe I wouldn't be in this mess with Hannah. Maybe I'd have Kyra. I've seen the way she watches me. I can see the need and want in her eyes for me. I know it because it's reflected in mine, but she needs more than I can give. She *deserves* more than I can give. Derek's the same; what could I offer either of them? Sex, that's it.

I need a drink; I can't deal with this shit. How fucking dare he, all of sudden after six long years, decide to tell me he's into dudes. Why am I feeling this way now? Is it a game? Trickery of some kind? Fuck I'm losing it; I'm boarding the crazy train.

"Jasp, we're heading home. I need to go over the other contracts tomorrow with you, okay?" Sammy says, putting a stop to my internal war.

"Sure, I'll come into office tomorrow." I smile and wrap River in a hug. I watch Derek whisper something in Kyra's ear and a twinge in my stomach makes me hate myself for feeling these things. I refuse to care about them other than as friends, and I refuse to be jealous of what they could be working towards. I don't do emotions. I just need to get laid. I just need to get him out of my head. When I move out, it'll all go back to how it was.

"Jasp! Jasp, you coming in or what?" I look to Derek, then to Sammy's car pulling off the drive. I had been thinking so hard I zoned out *again.*

"You okay?" Derek asks.

"No, I'm not okay." I barge past him back into the house, his heavy footfalls following behind me. He's close and I can't think straight.

"Jasp?"

I turn, pointing my finger at him. "Don't, Derek. I can't fucking deal with this shit anymore. I'm going out. I need to get laid," I say, walking back the way I came, towards the front door.

I gasp for breath as my back impacts against the wall, the air leaving my lungs on contact. Derek's frame crowds my body, his brown eyes searching mine. I can smell him. I can feel his body pressed against mine, and my dick hardens, a rush of saliva feeding my mouth at the sight of his lips so close to mine.

"You won't leave this house to go fuck some slut just because you want to fuck me and you're feeling weird about it."

"I don't want to fuck you," I lie. His smirk makes me squirm, *fucking squirm! Me?* I'm the one who makes people squirm. How has he turned the tables on me like this?

"Oh, God," I breathe when his hand grasps my erection through my jeans. My body stiffens. *Derek is holding my dick, Derek is holding my dick.*

"Tell that to your cock, Jasp." His smirk grows with satisfaction at the effect he has on me.

I push him away and he lets me. "Fuck you!" I nudge past him and head for the door. I find myself pushed up against the wall again, face first this time. His hand rests on the back of my head, pinning my face, my body covered with his. I feel his erection push against my ass.

"Yes, Jasp. Fuck me." He grabs the hand I try to use to push myself from the wall and pins it behind my back like he's arresting me. "You need me to take the lead and show you what you want? Then I will because there's no way you're giving this lust and anger to some cheap unworthy slut. It's mine and I want it!" he growls in my ear, his teeth grazing the lobe. My heart races, my breath coming in fast gasps. I'm propelled around to face him; he overpowers me with ease. I can't look away from him once our eyes meet; the intensity in his gaze leaves me breathless.

"You want this and I know you're struggling, so I'll make it easier. Don't fucking move."

I couldn't even if I tried. I'm frozen with the confusion of what's happening; from the built up tension making my cock ready to explode. He reaches for my zipper and my hands dart out to stop him reflexively.

"Put your fucking hands back on the wall, Jasp, palm

flat."

I comply. The vibration of nerves wrack my body, the anticipation driving me to embrace what's happening. His hands flick the buttons open on my jeans and the cold air hits my sensitive cock, making me inhale sharply. I don't wear underwear so my dick is exposed to his greedy gaze. His eyes gloss over with a glassy sheen. The look makes me so horny, I want to roar like a fucking beast. He slips my jeans down below my ass cheeks. *Oh fuck, oh fuck, oh fuck.*

He reaches out, his warm, huge hand grasping and closing around my heavy cock. I can't look away, I can't move. All I can do is watch and feel. It's like I'm here, but I'm not. My mind can't comprehend what's happening and my dick doesn't care, it just wants relief from this build up, from teetering on the edge of this fucking lust it's been feeling for Derek. He strokes upwards, gaining a groan from the back of my throat. "You have a pretty cock, Jasp," he tells me, licking his lips. Fucking pretty? Is he mocking me? No man wants *pretty* associated with them.

He laughs at the distaste clearly apparent on my face. "It's divine, Jasp. So fucking pretty. I want to lick every impressive inch of it."

Fuck me! I can't take much more if he keeps talking like that with his firm grip stroking up my shaft. I'll blow. *Oh God, he's dropping to his knees, oh God.*

I swallow the objection wanting to roar from my mouth as my mind tells me this is not me, but when his full lips kiss the tip of my cock, words aren't coherent, thoughts disappear and reasoning flies out the window. Nothing else matters except him opening up and taking me into his mouth. My hips jerk forward, nudging his lips, and he grins and opens his mouth wider, his tongue swiping out to taste the pre-come glistening on the head. He moans and sucks me into his mouth; my head falls back with a thud against the wall as he takes my full nine inches down the back of his throat.

"FUCK!" His suction and depth is the best I've ever felt; his hands massage my balls as he sucks up and down my shaft, tasting, teasing and driving me insane. I can't control my urges, I'm going to blow. I try to pull out.

"I'm gonna come, I'm gonna come," I moan, trying to warn him. He grips me by the ass cheeks and sucks at me like a starving man being given food for the first time. My balls tighten up, my stomach contracts, and my cock empties down the back of his throat. He moans in pleasure, in sync with my own moans.

The knock at the door brings reality speeding into my brain at a rapid rate, leaving me feeling dizzy and sick. *What the fuck did I just let happen?*

I push him away, more aggressive than I should. I whip my jeans up and rush towards the stairs, taking them two at a time to my room. I slam the door and throw myself on the bed.

What the fuck?! Derek just sucked me off and I liked it. Ha! Like is a fucking understatement. I have never been that turned on in my whole life. God, will Sammy know? Will he see it on my face? Will he still want to be my family, my brother?

Shit! I'm a twenty-eight-year-old and acting like a mixed up teen.

I hear Kyra's laughter and my body tenses. I jump from the bed to see what's going on. When I come down into the lobby, she's standing with Derek, whispering shit to her again.

"What the fuck? I thought you left?" She starts and looks up at me. He glares at me for my tone, but I don't care. He has me all twisted up, and two minutes ago had me throat deep in his mouth. My dick stirs when he drops a small kiss to her lips.

Fuck, will she smell me on him, taste me on his lips? She blushes and offers him a timid smile before looking back to me and holding up her purse.

"I forgot my purse. Sammy just brought me back to grab it." I nod my head. "You okay? You look a little flushed," she asks, stepping towards me.

I react without thinking, jumping backwards, nearly falling on my ass when I stumble up the step I'm on. I just can't have her look at me too closely. She'll smell the sex on me, see the glint, the flush, the guilt. It's all there in my eyes, I know it is.

She steps back, holding her hands up. "Wow, maybe you should go lie down."

I chew my bottom lip with my teeth and turn to go back up the stairs. I hear muffled voices talking, but I just need to be away from them both.

Derek

I see Kyra out and wave to Sammy, then close the door and collapse against it. I can't believe what just happened. I've never been that turned on in my life, and to finally just taste him succeeded any fantasy I ever had. Kyra turning back up should have been taken as a sign. We're heading towards dating, yet here I was with Jasper, and I can't regret or feel bad about it. I've wanted him for too long to deny myself when I know he wants me, too. Granted, my feelings run deeper than his ever could, but the lust, so powerful in his eyes, was magnetising.

I take the stairs in a hurried pace only to stand outside Jasper's door for a good five minutes before knocking.

"Jasp?"

The silence is deafening. I know he'll be freaking out. What if he moves out sooner? What if he's packing now?

"I'm going to bed, Derek. I have to work early tomorrow."

I exhale, holding my hands against the frame and resting my forehead against the door. "You don't want to talk about what happened?"

I hear him shuffling around before the door springs open without warning, making me nearly stumble forward. His hair is in disarray and the look in his eyes tells me there's a war raging inside him. I don't want to push him into discussions he's not ready for as much as I want him. I love him enough not to demand things he's struggling with; he needs to come to me.

"I don't want to talk right now, Der. I don't even know what the fuck to say."

I tilt my head to the side to study his face as his eyes drop to his feet. I take his chin between my thumb and forefinger, lifting his face, so I can look in his blue depths. "Don't say anything. Get some rest. It's just me, Jasp. I've waited this long, so take all the time you need to realise it's okay to feel what you're feeling."

His brow furrows. "Is it?"

I slip my hand around the nape of his neck and bring him forward. I gently press my lips to his, then pull back. "Does it feel okay?"

His eyes have closed and I need to walk away or I won't be able to stop what happens.

"Night, Der," he calls out as I walk to my room. I stop in the doorway and glimpse back at him briefly before shutting the door.

* * * * *

I wake to the smell of coffee and the sun streaming through my blinds like a laser beam, making me squint. I had lain awake most of the night replaying everything that happened; the feel of his smooth cock as it slid down my throat, his slightly bitter, but divine taste on my tongue, firing off on my taste buds. I wanted to devour him; I wanted every inch under my tongue.

I look at the bedside clock. 9:15. *Shit!* I overslept, or under slept, considering I only got around three hours in total. I notice the coffee mug steaming with a note next to it.

I made coffee as you weren't up, and if you had a restless night like me, you needed the lie-in.

J

The cup is hot; he's only just been in here. I sip the coffee and try not to gag. Jasper just can't brew coffee. I'm used to the tar at the office, though, so I manage to get it down. The fact that he hadn't just left without a word is a big positive. I feel lighter today. I finally released something from the steel trap inside me and it feels good, really good.

I have a quick workout before showering and heading out. I stop off at the studio to check in on the girls and find Jasper there, talking in hushed tones with River. My head swims with the possibility of him actually telling her about what happened.

She spots me coming towards them, her eyes flaring fleetingly before muttering to Jasper, who looks over his shoulder and shifts away from her.

"Yeah, so that's what Sammy said. I'll catch you later," he tells her, his voice a little higher than it should be. He turns to me. "Oh, hey. I didn't see you come in. I'm just leaving."

I put his weird behaviour down to the fact that he's still struggling with what went down, or rather, who. I smirk at my inner thoughts and watch his footing stumble. It feels good to have such an effect on him. Jasper is beyond good-looking. He's molded from the highest quality God had to offer. Even his hair is perfect—soft and shiny—and his eyes are crystallised sky blue orbs. He works hard to maintain his trim perfect physique.

"Guys, what's with the glaring?"

I pull my eyes from his to River's; her brows are nearly in her hairline.

"Nothing, he ruined coffee this morning," I stutter, flinching at my lame explanation.

"You must have had something in your mouth that's thrown your taste buds off." Jasper sneers, quirking an eyebrow before walking out and leaving my jaw on the floor.

"What was that?" River asks, tapping my chest.

"Nothing. What was he doing here?"

Her eyes look at anything but me. "Oh, just checking in for Sammy. He was going to get them lunch." I don't question her blatant dishonesty as I look around for Kyra.

"She's gone to an audition with a student."

"What? Who?"

She gives me an *are you kidding* look. "Kyra. Let's not pretend you came here to watch my ass dance around this place."

A laugh rips from my chest.

She rises up on her tiptoes to drop a kiss to my cheek.

God, I'm happy. This is a new feeling for me. I wasn't a depressed asshole before, but I wasn't the happy-go-lucky type, either. But I feel warmth in my chest, a little light shining on the dark past that lives inside me.

"Crap, Derek," River calls after me as I push the door to leave. She jogs towards me. "Jasp left his wallet on the counter. Can you drop it over to him?"

"Didn't you say he's gone for food? Call him, I'll take it to where he's at."

She shifts from foot to foot, then twirls a strand of her hair. "I called. He's gone back to work."

She can't be serious; there is no way she called him. I grab the wallet and point my finger at her. "I'm a detective, and even if I wasn't, I know you like I know the back of my hand, Riv! I don't like that you're lying, but I trust that it's need to know, so I'll let it go. But in future just say it's private instead of this"—I wave my hand up and down in front of her—"bullshit! You can't lie for shit."

I stop for some coffee and grab a few sandwiches to take to Jasper and Sammy. Sammy is looking over a Maserati when I arrive; a sleek, silver driver's heaven in a compact, beautiful package.

"Nice. Who owns this?" I ask as I admire the high quality leather interior.

"We just secured a new contract with Pyerade Construction to service all their company cars." He beams.

That's a huge company and an amazing contract to land. I know Jasper sorts that side of things and the pride booms in my chest.

"This is not a company car," I state. "I nearly bought one of these." I skim my hand over the roof.

"You flash bastard. This, we shouldn't be touching. It's insured with Maserati, but the guy who owns the company called in a favour." Sammy eyeballs the bag in my hand. "You brought lunch, what's going on?"

"Ha ha, I bought coffee, too. I was at the studio. Riv said Jasp left his wallet and was meant to grab lunch for you."

He shakes his head and tugs a rag in his pocket. "Stevey, give it what it needs, but keep it out of the service manual," he calls over his shoulder, striding towards my car, opening the door and bringing out the coffees. "Come on then." He gestures towards the office. "Fuck knows where Jasper's head's at. He's acting shifty as shit."

He pulls open the glass door; I grab it and follow behind him. He hands me my coffee cup and slides Jasper's on the counter. "JASP!" he shouts, banging on Jasper's office door.

"What's up?" comes a reply from behind the still-closed door.

Sammy looks over at me, raising his hands in a "what the fuck" gesture. "Open the door, asshole. Your boyfriend just arrived."

He's laughing as he says it, but hearing that leave his lips makes me drop my cup. He jumps to avoid the hot splash from the impact as the main door swings open, the same time Jasper's office door opens. His eyes grow like saucers when he sees me standing there.

"Hi, Jasper," a male, but feminine voice purrs from behind me.

I look over my shoulder at a skinny blond guy. He must be in his early twenties; he's wearing skin tight black jeans, a purple shirt tucked in with a pink bow tie. "Oh hello, tall, dark, and handsome." He accentuates the *ome*, scanning me from top to toe, his eyes lingering on my ass.

"Denny, just drop the package off and piss off will you."

"Ohhh, sorry, Jasper. Who else has *not* got up your ass today?"

It happens quickly, and if it wasn't for Jasper slipping on the river of coffee at my feet, he wouldn't have lost his footing and toppled into me, giving me the advantage to grip onto him and stop him landing a right hook to this kid.

Sammy rushes forwards to help grab Jasper, and slips in the coffee, too, landing in a heap. "Motherfucker!" he bellows, the sound echoing around the room.

"Argh, I was joking, I was joking!" the kid screeches, backing away and holding his hands up.

Jasper leans over my arm, pointing his finger at him. "You go too fucking far, Denny."

"Just go, Denny," Sammy growls from the floor. "Seriously, what the fuck?" He groans, rubbing his thigh.

"He crossed a line, Sammy. I want him gone!" Jasper pulls from me, the heat from his body still warming my chest.

"Get the fucking mop and stop being so dramatic. He's always like that with you. You've been acting fucking weird or guilty or some shit." Sammy stands up and the coffee has completely drenched him. "What have you done?"

Jasper's hands go to his hips, his head bowed. "Why do you assume I've done something? You really have a shitty opinion of me."

"Opinion, or years of friendship to back up facts?"

He moves forward and shoves Sammy who stumbles backwards. "Hey, hey," I say, grabbing Jasper. Sammy glares back at him with a raised brow. Jasper shakes me off, then goes back in his office and slams the door. The whole frame shakes from the force, the sound piercing the air.

"I told you he was acting weird. I need to go change. Talk to him, will you? Find out what's going on."

I wait until Sammy is out of sight before entering. The handle gives way under my hand and I slip in and close it behind me. He sits at his desk, his elbows resting on it and his hands holding his head.

"Jasp?"

His breathing is ragged and in a quick movement, he's up out of his chair and in my space, his eyes burning into mine. "What the fuck are you doing to me? Why can't I stop the craving?"

His lips smash against mine, his hands gripping my hair in an almost painful grasp. His tongue seeks entry and I'm done letting him lead. I grip his hair and tug his face from mine, his mouth is all swollen and glowing with a red tinge, and his eyes have melted into pools of lust. I bite down on his lip drawing a deep groan from him.

I release the bruised lip and swipe my tongue over it to soothe it. "Because every craving needs to be fed." I force his lips back to mine, consuming them. I take every tongue caress, every tooth graze across my lips, and every tug on my hair, and the feel of his tight, hard body pushing into mine.

His phone ringing is a distant hum in the background. *Bang, bang, bang!* "Answer your phone, asshole," Sammy shouts through the door.

Jasper wrenches away from me as the answer machine kicks in and Hannah's voice washes through the room, dousing the fire that engulfed it moments before.

"Jasper, it's Hannah. You weren't answering your cell. Surprise, surprise." She breathes down the line causing a dreadful noise to fill the room. "I came home earlier than expected and wanted you to come here tonight to talk some things over. Call me."

He stares at the phone, not speaking or moving, and I

exit without a word.

Sammy sits there at the reception desk expectantly in fresh jeans and polo shirt. "I thought you were going home to change?" I ask.

He scoffs and goes back to his computer. "When you work here, you're used to being covered in crap from one thing or another. I keep clothes here." He looks to me, then to Jasper's closed door. "Did you find out what's eating him?"

I close my eyes at his choice of words and shake my head. "Just this Hannah crap. I need to go." I lift my chin and he returns the gesture.

The breeze hits my heated flesh as I step outside. Why did she have to call in that moment; making us both remember that she exists and how everything is going to change soon?

* * * * *

I walk into the precinct; the flurry of activity all around me draws me from my thoughts. I recognise Johnny Marten sitting at Hans' desk in handcuffs.

"Two weeks you've been out of prison. What have you done this time?"

He scowls at Hans, then looks up at me. "Like I told this asshole, I was set up."

Hans bites into an apple; the juice squirts from his mouth and sprays some file on his desk. "Who would want to set you up and in the process lose their coke, you dumb fuck?" Hans kicks the leg of Johnny's chair.

"Look, police harassment!" he shouts at me.

"Tell it to a judge, Johnny, and to your cell mate." I point to my office for Hans to follow.

"Get him in an interview room, Jones," Hans calls out, shutting the door behind him.

"Update on the suspect?" He bites more from his apple, then tosses it into my trash can. "What's with the apple? I don't think I've ever seen you eat anything that's not a pastry."

He turns his nose up. "The wife has cut me off until I lose a few pounds for our vacation."

"Update." I can't even respond to that.

"They moved him from ICU. He's stable, but in an induced coma until the swelling reduces, and then it's a waiting game. He may never wake up and if he does, he may not be like he was."

I squint my eyes at him. "A stalking, woman molesting abuser?"

He rolls his eyes. "He may be brain damaged; they don't know the extent of his brain injury yet."

"Fine, just keep me informed."

My phone chirps with a text alert and I wave Hans out.

Kyra and Dawn are at the club tonight. Jasp was supposed to take them home afterwards, but he said he's busy now and to text you. R

I hated her going to these clubs, but she loved going and letting her hair down every now and then, and how could I deny her? Dancing was expression for River, her way of pouring everything she was feeling out, releasing her emotions, and she was breathtaking. Dawn was a helper at the studio and sometimes tagged along with River, now it was Kyra.

Time, Riv?

11? R

Fine, I will come in for them.

They will meet you outside. R

I WILL come IN for them!!!!

Ok DAD! . R

I can picture her giggling at her own text when she typed that. It was bad enough Kyra and Dawn were going alone. The last thing I wanted was them waiting in the street at that time of night.

Kyra

Sweaty bodies gyrate too close for comfort. I hate these people trying to dance so close to us. I need to move, breathe and live the music through movement. Dawn is enjoying herself. When River insisted I come here with her, all paid for by her as a thank you for the work I've taken on, I couldn't refuse. You don't turn down a thank you, especially considering who it was from and her excitement in giving me it.

I feel like I owe her the thanks, though. I love my new position, and River letting me stay with her and Sammy really warms my heart. They're all becoming so important to me, and I adore Mikey.

Sammy is so in love with River, and it's special to witness that so closely. It leaves an ache in my chest, though. I know Derek and I are going slow, and because I'm falling for both him and Jasper, going slow is a good thing. The tension between them is growing by the day. Jasper seems so tightly wound. I sense his eyes on me before I see him, *Derek*, the outbreak of goose bumps raising the tiny hairs all over my body, the rhythm of my heartbeats picking up, the air thickening all around me, and the heavy haze of lust clinging to my skin.

I'm swaying my hips in time to the music, the sweat lightly beading my exposed skin. His scent immerses me as his arms snake around my middle. "Hey, Beauty," he breathes against my ear. "You ready?"

I try not to slump my shoulders at the disappointment from him wanting to leave already and not dance with me. Dawn leans forward to tell me her boyfriend is here. I turn to face Derek; he looks gorgeous in the dimmed light. "I'm just taking her over to her boyfriend. Can you grab my coat from our table, then I'm ready to go." He nods in agreement.

I take Dawn's arm and weave through the crowd of bodies. "You wait till you see him, he is d.i.v.i.n.e!"

I had been hearing about her new boyfriend for the last week and I already know the details of his manhood.

"There he is!" She points, kisses my cheek and bounds over to him. He's good-looking from what I can make out from this distance, but one thing for sure, his eyes are undressing me and making my intuition spike. He's bad news and will no doubt break her heart. A shiver racks my body when his eyes don't leave me. I glare and scrunch my nose at him before turning and searching for Derek. He's not at the table where my coat was, so I make my way outside. The bite of the cooler air chills the skin on my arms and I rub them to keep warm. I spot his car, but not him. I cross the road to where he's parked and lean against the car to wait for him. I'm going to kiss him and maybe ask if I can stay at his place again, like before. I go over in my mind what I can say, working up the courage I'll need, when a body crowds me, enclosing all around me; it's Derek. I would know his scent anywhere.

"What are you doing out here?" he growls, stepping back. He holds his phone up. "Where's your cell phone? I was calling it. No answer, Kyra?" He used my real name and I gulp down the lump in my throat. "I was worried sick and searching for you like a madman. You know how dangerous it is for you to be out her alone?" His voice had risen with every word. I'm humiliated that he's shouting at me in the street as a few club stragglers are looking over at us. I glance down at my dress; it's conservative compared to the way some of the girls dressed in the club.

"I'm sorry, I couldn't find you," I mutter.

"Get in the car."

I slip into the seat when he opens the door, and buckle myself in. I fight the urge to cry, but I feel like the tears are going to spring free. The car shifts with his weight as he gets into the driver's seat. He exhales and grips the wheel tightly as he leans forward, resting his forehead against it. "I'm sorry, Beauty."

The first tear betrays me and leaks down my cheek, leaving a damp trail in its wake.

"Oh God, are you crying?" he sounds remorseful, so I shake my head, but the little hiccup escapes my chest, exploiting my lie.

He reaches for me, scooping me into his lap. I curl around him and gently cry into his shoulder. "Please don't cry. I'm sorry. I nearly had a heart attack when I couldn't find you. I'm sorry."

I relax against him, the heat from his body warming my own.

We stay like this until my tears dry. He places me back into my seat and buckles my belt, smiling at me.

"I'm going to take you to Riv's."

"Okay," I whisper. The earlier confidence to tell him I wanted to stay with him was carried away in the breeze.

The drive is done with just the radio breaking the silence. Derek pulls up and steps from the car, coming round to open my door. He offers his hand and I clasp it, welcoming his strong support. He grips the nape of my neck once I'm standing in front of him.

He studies my face, his eyes softening. "I'm sorry, Beauty, okay?"

I nod, lost in the gentle vulnerability searching my eyes. He leans forward and drops a kiss to my head. "River is twitching the curtain, so you better go in." He smiles, looking up at the window. I follow his gaze and he's right; the curtain moves and a giggle escapes me. His laughter joins mine.

"She's like a mom on prom night." I chuckle.

"I wouldn't be bringing you home if it was prom night." He winks.

I bite my lip and take my coat from him. "Thanks for the ride."

Jasper

Hannah looks fine, happy and glowing. She was all smiles and pleasantries when I came in. She told me she's feeling more positive about everything, and maybe we should think about putting down roots in the housing market. I agreed and went to the bathroom to make sure I didn't vomit the self-pity I was feeling all over her cream rug.

Her suitcase is on the bathroom floor, open, and usually I would never look through her stuff, but the open condom wrapper just slightly visible has me throwing her shit on the floor and finding her box of condoms half empty. I knew she was fucking someone else. The signs were literally staring me in the face in the form of her mother when she was supposed to be away with her. The anger at her fucking someone while pregnant with my baby is immense. I crush the box in my hand and go confront her.

I walk into the living room to find her lying on the couch laughing at a *Friends* rerun and she's rubbing her stomach. The anger leaves me as quickly as it came. What the fuck does it matter? We both know this isn't love. All I can think about is when I can get back to Derek; every thought is consumed by him. What would shouting and demanding answers to questions I already had the answers to achieve? Nothing had really changed, or would; we're a business marriage and that's that.

She must sense me because she looks over at me. "You okay?" she asks, seeming genuinely curious.

"Yeah, fine."

"Well, you don't have to stay, Jasper. I'm having an early night anyway."

Fuck! The endorphins from the happiness and relief at her words make me feel like I'm floating. I force myself towards her, lean down, and plant a chaste kiss to her head before grabbing my keys.

* * * * *

The place is quiet when I get home. I feel my whole body pulsing with need and Derek's not even here. The front door shifts open behind me. He steps into the lobby, the light from a side table illuminating him. He freezes when he sees me.

"Something inside me has an inconsolable addiction to you. I'm struggling to fucking fight it," I tell him.

He walks past me and takes the stairs. I follow; he stops just beside the wall next to his room, his allure pouring from him in waves. This wasn't who I used to being, but he has changed me, or bewitched me. I'm under his spell and the link is too strong to fight when I look over at him.

He's the master and I am being summoned. I can't refuse it, nor control the pulsating need for him. He's beckoning me to him and I'm going to him willingly, captivated by his magnetism.

I go to him, leaving everything I was behind with every step I take in his direction. My body hums with electricity, lightening the atmosphere with its energy and vibrating me with need; I'm running on the pure adrenaline of this moment. There's no gentle, no waiting, he rips my shirt down the middle, my stomach tensing as the cool air hits my heated skin. My breathing is as erratic as my heartbeat.

His mouth crashes down onto mine and I let go. I release all the want and lust I have kept prisoner inside me as I unleash the sexual need I have for him.

My tongue clashes with his in a battle for dominance, his frame crowds mine, encompassing me in everything he is, his scent mingling with mine, his sweat blending with my own, our essence fusing and becoming one with every breath we share.

His hands rip open my jeans, tugging them. They drop to my ankles and my hard cock springs free to welcome the hand that grasps it. His firm grip tugs on me aggressively, pulling a ragged groan from the back of my throat.

His chest pins mine as his tongue wins our battle and devours my mouth. His other hand grips the back of my neck, controlling the movements of my head. His firm strokes of my cock make me ready to explode.

His lips travel up my cheek to my ear. "Bedroom, Jasp, now," he growls, releasing me from his hold.

I kick my jeans free and walk to his bedroom, the nerves rattling around in my stomach, the anticipation ruling every other emotion. I'm shoved onto the bed from behind, his body comes down from above me and crushes me under his weight. He's stripped and I feel every naked inch of his powerful body. His cock is resting between my ass cheeks. I gasp to fill my lungs with much needed oxygen as his lips trace hot needy kisses over my shoulders, teeth nipping at my skin.

His lips travel the length of my spine, his bite going deeper into my flesh when he reaches my ass. This is new and

I'm nervous. This is it, no going back once I do this. He has me pinned. He's changed me.

His tongue dips in between the seam of my ass, stroking my anus and I jerk forward, but his hand grasps my hips to hold me there. He begins again, swiping his tongue up and around the opening. It feels so fucking good and I groan into the mattress. The pleasure is too much.

His hands shift to my ass cheeks, separating them for his greedy mouth. His tongue probes the hole; I fucking can't take this, it's all too much. The pleasure, the reluctance to accept it, to accept the need my body so clearly wants, and it's all his fucking fault.

I jackknife upwards in a movement too quick for him to foresee or stop. He falls behind me on to the bed and I grab him and pin him down, the anger and lust combining into a frenzy. "You want this Derek, you can fucking have it," I growl above him. I position my dick between his ass cheeks and plunge forward; no lube, no foreplay and he is so fucking tight I nearly blow my load straight inside him.

His roar matches my own. I power forward with no mercy, fucking him with everything I have. I grasp his hips and plunge forward and back, smashing myself into him, my balls slapping against his. I reach around, grasping his heavy cock in my hand and stroke him with every erratic thrust. "Is this what you wanted?"

I continue the assault, his growling making me thrust deeper and stroke his cock faster. "Yes!"

"Is this what you wanted? Me fucking you, Derek?"

I fuck him until my legs go weak and I feel the familiar build tingle up my spine; my balls tightening up, releasing my come like an explosion, hot and pulsating into his ass as his cock explodes in my hand. "Fuck!" We groan in unison as our lust fuelled frenzy reaches its conclusion, and then I collapse over him.

Derek

I feel his weight collapse on to me, his hot breath searing the skin on my shoulder, then the gentle shake of his chest and the warm wet drops. He's crying, and my insides crumble.

I had waited and wanted him for so long. The moment he entered me changed me, confirmed everything I knew I felt, but for him, it changed everything he ever knew about himself and the hot tears that struck my skin are like razor sharp knives.

I pushed him too fast, too far. I made him angry, fucked the lust out of him when I should have held him and showed him that it's okay to feel the way he does.

His small pants and gasps tighten my throat; I'm not a man of emotion, but fuck if he didn't bring emotion out of me. "Jasp," I murmur.

His body shifts from mine. I turn to see him now on his side, facing away from me with his arm covering his face, his body shaking with a sob.

"It's okay," I assure him over and over, bringing my body against his, cradling him against me. I gently lower his arm, his piercing blues look like crystals shining from the tears that coat them. I stroke the damp from his cheeks with the pad of my thumb. "It's okay, Jasp."

Leaning down, I brush my lips with his. His brow furrows and I feel the tension leave his body. My cock stiffens against him, still seeping from the release he had given me moments before. I watch acceptance flash in his eyes and then his hand reaches up to grasp my face, bringing his lips back to mine in a hungry kiss, his tongue massaging mine.

My hands roam his body, committing every dip and muscle into my memory. He is beautiful, God, like perfection, toned and sculpted. Tanned and smooth, tall perfection.

I drop my lips to the curve of his neck, biting my way along his shoulder. His ass grinds against me while my hands find his rock hard cock standing proud up his stomach. I stroke him gently, taking my time to worship him. He thrusts with my strokes, building momentum, building the fire that blazes inside us both. "More, Jasp. Fuck my hand. Give me your release."

His breathing picks up with his forward thrusts. I push against him, grinding my cock into the crease of his ass cheeks. "Oh fuck, I'm gonna come," he moans and I have to hold back my own release screaming at me to coat his skin with my scent, my essence.

I feel his body tense; his cock pulsates in my hand, then floods my fist with his seed. I capture it in my hand and pump until the last drops leave him. The air is thick with our body heat, the light mist of sweat clinging to our bodies, making us glide effortlessly against each other.

I use his come to coat my fingers, and then coat my cock, still slick from my own come. I rub his ass cheeks with my palm before slipping my finger against his tight ring, pushing past the muscle. His body tenses then relaxes as I pump in and out, still grinding my body with his.

My lips seek his, mashing together in an unhurried

intimate dance of lips and tongues. I push a second finger inside him, stroking in delicate movements to stretch and ready him.

I pull my fingers free and line my cock up against him. "You ready, Jasp?"

He pushes his ass against me, giving me the signal he wants this. I slowly push in, our mixed come giving me the help I need to slip in past the tight muscle. He's so fucking tight, squeezing my shaft in his heat and I have to pause and take a few deep breaths. I control my breathing and the urge to come and relax against his back. My arm comes around his chest, my lips against his ear and I thrust forward, relishing in his moan of pleasure.

"Jasp, you feel incredible."

I pull back, then thrust harder. He's everything I imagined and more. I love him and I have him here in my arms, my cock buried inside him, and in this moment, he is mine.

We move in sync, his body against mine, and our movements pick up speed and need as our bodies build to climax. I power forward, rocking into him and grip his chest tight. I bite down on his shoulder in bliss of our climax.

It shatters me, roaring from me in a tidal wave of built up longing for him. Nothing can ever take this moment from me and as I pump my release inside him, I feel nirvana for the first time in my life. Mya's death, my Mom's abandonment, River's trauma, being shot. Nothing mattered; nothing could undermine how amazing this moment feels. He has given me freedom, peace for the first time since Mya, and I fall more in love with him, more than ever before.

* * * * *

I wake from the heat against my body. It's new for me to wake with someone against me in my bed. Jasper's scent is emanating from him, occupying my senses and thoughts; I know he'll be sore today, so my thickening cock against him makes me groan in frustration. I trace kisses along his shoulder, arousing him from slumber.

He grinds into me making me catch my breath in a gasp. "Shower, Jasp," I groan and thrust against him once before making my way to the shower.

My body has an entrancing ache all over, making me relive the night before's incredible development.

I turn the water on and step into the spray. The water massages my sensitive skin, the steam soothing the ache in my muscles. I feel the breeze of the door opening before his presence suffocates all my senses and I welcome the strength of it.

I turn to face him, the water leaving a silk like glow to his skin; his eyes are fixated on my growing erection standing to welcome him. His hand reaches and closes around it, the heat and feel of his palm sealed around my shaft makes my head roll back on my shoulders.

His movement is hesitant at first; his breathing is increasing with his fist strokes and I force myself to look at him; the steam billowing around his perfect form, his crystal blues dreamily regarding my cock as his fist fucks me.

I look down to watch his thumb slowly swipe the beading come at the tip. He rubs the pad of his thumb in a circular movement over the head as his palm stokes my shaft in firm powerful thrust. I move my hips to meet his movements, the intensity growing and tightening my balls; his hand reaches out to cup them, gently squeezing.

I feel the tingle race up my spine; his abs tighten as the

string of hot come coats Jasper's navel, the sight of my seed on his skin making me come harder, spiralling out, marking him as mine. In this moment he is all mine.

Jasper

It's just something I need to get out my system, we both said that the first night after the shower, but all week was the same routine. Crawl out of Derek's bed, fuck in the shower, go to work, avoid all eye contact and any other contact with Sammy, go check on Hannah, leave as quickly as I came. Go home and fuck Derek.

He's an addiction I never knew I would be hooked on, but I am. I'm hooked and flying high on the feelings pulsating through me. I feel alive; every molecule comes to life when he's touching me. I feel wanted in a completely different way to anything I've ever experienced before him and it's scary as fuck and soothing all at the same time.

Sammy knows something is off with me. We've never had a rift between us before. I'm just absolutely terrified that he'll see the facts in my eyes and the thought of him judging me and changing how he feels about me is something I'm not willing to risk.

Sammy isn't homophobic and I'm not gay, but the fact it's Derek, and then there's Kyra and Hannah. None of them need to know. I'll still be marrying Hannah and then my baby will come along, and everything will change again.

I slump into the mattress as my thoughts sour my mood, draining me. I fucking hate the mess I got myself into. The alert tone on my laptop notifies me my dad is Skyping me. I click accept and see the frosted white tips of my dad's once brown mop of hair. His eyes scan the screen; he has lines around his eyes that show the toll life has had on him, but that doesn't detract from the fact he is a handsome man.

"Hey, son." He waves.

"Hey, Pop." I shift the screen so I'm visible to him on his.

"You're looking well."

"Thanks, Pop, you too. So what's new with you?"

I see something cross his features, but it's gone before I can identify it. "I was thinking of coming for a visit in a couple of weeks."

I'm twenty-eight, but I'm still a son and I miss him. "That would be great, Dad. I actually have somethings to talk to you about."

He silently observes me before grinning. "That you do, son. Looking forward to seeing you. I'll email you with confirmed dates."

"Okay, sounds good."

"Great. Well, take care, and Jasp… That's a good look on you."

"What is?"

"Content, happy."

I adjust the screen, so he can't see the blush and guilt taking over my face. I'm turning into a bloody woman. *Me, blushing.* But he's right; I've never felt more content or happy than when I'm with Derek.

"Bye Jasp, I love you, son."

"Love you too, Dad. Bye."

I disconnect the call. Derek is working a new case, so he asked me to take Kyra apartment hunting. It'll be the first time seeing her since I freaked out a week ago. Derek is still acting overprotective of her wellbeing despite the fact that the creep who was preying on young women, including her, has now been caught.

I'm pleased, but also have a slight twinge of jealousy; in which direction, I'm not sure. Spending time with Kyra is always a test for me. Like Derek, she has an enticement that draws me in. I always feel like I can be me when I'm with her. She doesn't scrunch her nose up when I swear, or roll her eyes at my jokes. She just gets me and laughs along beside me. She is a rare find like River: kind, caring, loving, passionate, and beautiful. Beyond beautiful.

"Jasp, we're here," River calls up the stairs.

I pocket my wallet and keys, and make my way down to them. I didn't know River was going to come in. I thought she was just dropping Kyra off. I feel the nerves bustling in my veins; I try to shake it off, but River, like Sammy, is observant and when it comes to me, reads me like a book.

She's already quirking her brow at me as I come down to greet them. She looks behind me, then up the stairs. "You have someone up there?"

I notice Kyra's smile fall from her pretty face, her eyes going big and round. "You've been around Sammy too long. You think really shitty of me, River."

"You just look glowy and guilty, baby, which I know comes after dirty sex." She winks. It's my turn to scrunch my nose. River is hot, and as a male, I can appreciate that. I also had a very brief sexual encounter with her years ago when Sammy made me silence her moans with my tongue in her mouth, but that was a lifetime ago and she's my family now, so the thought of Sammy violating her in all the filthy ways I knew he would, weren't images I wanted.

Her mouth pops open. "You scrunched your nose at me!"

"I don't want to think about you and Sammy doing dirty sex. You're a mom."

She puts her hands on her hips and glares at me. "You are unbelievable."

I grin. "I know." I waggle my eyebrows.

"And there he is." Shaking her head, she turns from us. "Have fun," she calls over her shoulder.

I turn to Kyra. Her red locks bundled on top of her head have a few strands falling into her face, and her pouty, suckable lips have a gloss over them like an invitation to taste them. Fuck it. Five minutes and I was already at half-mast.

"Thanks for doing this, Jasper. I told Derek I could go on my own, but you know how he gets," she mumbles, handing over the property list.

"You know I don't mind, Ky. Come on, let's find you a place."

Her light foot falls follow behind me.

* * * * *

The first place is a little small, but the area seems nice and the neighbour is friendly when slipping me her number as soon as Kyra's back is turned.

"We offer amenities with the price. It's semi furnished, and a deposit is required. Feel free to look around," the middle aged estate agent tells us, her smile as false as her tits.

"Thanks." Kyra tucks a fallen strand of hair behind her ear. "What do you think?"

I look round at the old as fuck couch and the amateur paint work. I could fuck her on that breakfast bar. I walk to the bedroom; the bed dominates, leaving a four foot border. It has a slated headboard; I could tie her to that and explore every inch of that untouched body.

Oh, God! The thought of being the man to discover those hidden delights. The bathroom door is open, showing the medium sized shower cubicle. Images of Derek wet, glistening and hard as rock from this morning filter in. *Fuck!* Sammy and River are right, that is all I'm about.

"Jasp, what do you think?" Derek's image fades as Kyra speaks.

"It's small and Derek would kick my ass if I let you have something that's smaller than what you're already in."

She looks around and shrugs. "It's a better area."

"Let's look at the others, Ky."

The next place is well-maintained. The kitchen is clean and a good size; the bedroom could fit me and Derek in here with her. I check the closet space.

A high pitched scream resonates off the walls. I dart to her; she's standing on the kitchen counter with her arms wrapped tightly around her chest and she's doing the fucking two step with her feet.

She's pale white. "What happened?" I ask, out of breath from the heart attack and mini sprint to get to her.

"A mouse. Oh God, a mouse."

I look to where she's waving her hand and see the tiniest, little creature I've ever seen. It's quite fearless for something so small. I bend down to grab it and jump after another screech from Kyra. "Don't touch it." She over pronounces the word *it*.

"Everything okay in here?" the estate agent asks, coming in from outside after trying to give us privacy for viewing.

A tall shadow appears behind her, blocking the light from the doorway. "I heard the screams, did you find one?" The shadow belonging to a guy whose deep voice booms through the room, making the estate agent jump and stumble forward.

His face is covered in a full beard, his stomach big and round, shoving out the bottom of a t-shirt that clearly doesn't fit. He walks towards us and I instinctively stand to guard Kyra. His face softens when he looks down at my feet. "Aww there you are." He bends with a struggle and a grunt to scoop up the tiny animal. "I keep them as pets. Amber." He holds out the creature, causing a squeal from Kyra. "Amber's her mom. She got out and into the walls, I've been trying to find the litter. I heard her scream over the match, too."

He gestures around the room. "These walls are paper thin though, you hear everything…if you get me?" He jabs me in the arm and waggles his eyebrows.

I turn, grabbing the backs of Kyra's thighs. She yelps as I throw her over my shoulder and out of the apartment. The *clip-clop* of the estate agent's heels alerts me to her following. Kyra's ass is right next to my mouth and I have to fight the urge to bite it.

I open the car door, clasp her hips and slide her down my body. The friction sparking the already heated need I have for her. How can I have been sated by Derek this morning, and crave him like I do, yet here I am, totally engrossed in the feel of her tight, perfect body as it slides against mine?

"I'll meet you at the next property."

I look over my shoulder and shake my head. "No thanks, lady. We're done."

Her scowl and grunt as she walks away only confirms the decision that we need a new estate agent and budget. These places would never be okayed by Derek.

I help her into the car and go around to my side. Her scent has embedded itself in the interior, so I can smell her every time I get into the car and it signals my dick to pay my zipper a visit every time.

"So what now?"

"Now we go to my place, find a new estate agent, and eat dinner. I'm starving."

Her little smile lifts her lips, then drops abruptly. She chews her lip and twists her hair around her finger. "What is it, Ky?"

She drops her hair and shifts slightly to face the window. "I can't afford more than these places, Jasper. These were a push for me."

I can't look at her when she's all timid and vulnerable; it tugs on my inner man. It makes me want to ease her discomfort, tell her she deserves to live like a princess and will from this day forward because she's gorgeous and funny and every man's dream girl, but I can't say that, and I refuse to give way to the freight train of emotions trying to knock down the well-placed, strongly constructed wall I had secured since I was a boy. Derek has already taken a sledge hammer to it. I feel the cold seeping out whenever I'm with Derek or Kyra, and being replaced with warmth; warmth I shouldn't be feeling. But it's like nature—uncontrollable, powerful, and it doesn't show mercy.

Kyra

I can sense the change in Jasper. He's happier. I know Hannah is home, and maybe they're getting on better and he's making the effort. I hate it and I have no right to, but I feel things for him I never wanted to give permission to. He pulled it free with just his presence. He's a unique soul; he brings light with him wherever he goes. He can walk in a room and the air will be clearer, and the mood instantly brighter.

Some people are born to impact people, and that's what Jasper was born to do. He and Derek are an impossible choice, and one I don't need to make. Jasper isn't available, and if he was, how could I choose between them?

"You want me to make dinner?" he asks, opening the car door.

I hadn't realised we've arrived. "When you say make, you mean make the call?"

His smirk is a panty-melting, drool on chin, legs of jelly smirk. "Aww, you know me so well."

I'm surprised to see Derek sitting at the dining table when we come in. Jasper's steps falter when he notices him. "I thought you were working?"

Derek looks up at him and takes his time before replying like they're having a conversation through telepathy. "I got a break in the case; the suspect was picked up after a tip off that he was in a different state. They're transferring him here, so I can question him and make the formal charges." He looks over at me, his eyes lure me in and I find my feet moving towards him. "Hey, Beauty. How did the apartment hunt go?"

I drop my eyes from his, embarrassed by his question. I know he doesn't have to even think about money, so it isn't in his mind when wanting me to find a place.

"What's wrong?" Both he and Jasper ask in unison, stepping into my space and each other's. The air around us ignites in an instant; all of us have laboured breathing and I can't concentrate. They're blocking any reasonable thoughts with a lust haze, coating the room and fogging my mind.

Derek is the first to break the trance when he steps back and swipes a hand over his brow to wipe the sweat beading there.

"She needs a bigger budget. Those places are no better than what's she is in," Jasper informs him, making me uncomfortable. My place isn't the Ritz, but it's mine. I paid for everything inside it by myself.

"She doesn't need a budget, I already told her that. She just needs to like it and let me worry about the rest."

"Guys, I am in the room. Derek, I can't just do that. I wouldn't feel right about it."

He comes closer to me, wrapping me in his embrace. "Ky, I have the means and I want to. Don't overthink this please."

I'm not going to argue with him, knowing he's stubborn and will never let me win.

"Mmm, you cooked," Jasp blurts out like a five-year-old being told there's cake. The aroma of Italian tomato sauce fills the thickened air.

"Yes, sit. I'll serve up." Jasper rubs his stomach and grins while taking a seat at the table.

I didn't realise how hungry I was until I shovelled in the first spoonful of Derek's food. It's so good and I clear my plate, to his pleasure. Jasper cleared two. The conversation is easy, effortless.

"Show him some moves, Ky." Derek shakes his head at Jasper's suggestion. We've moved from the dining room to the lounge. Jasper has put on some music and is showing me a step routine River had taught him for her wedding. The way Derek watched him left me feeling like an intruder viewing an intimate moment only meant for the two of them, but then his gaze would shift to me and the same intensity would smoulder in his eyes.

"Fine. I'm going to bed then, you coming?" Both mine and Derek's heads snap to Jasper.

"I meant going. Are you going?"

"Yes, I am unless it's okay to invite myself to stay?" I giggle; the wine Derek gave me with dinner has left me slightly woozy.

"You never need an invite. You're always welcome," Derek tells me, resting his hand on my lower back and guiding me to the stairs. I murmur my goodnights and make my way to the room I use here.

I strip off my clothes and crawl into the plush comfort of the covers in just my underwear. My head rests against the plump fibre of the pillow and darkness chases me into slumber.

* * * * *

Movement outside my room has me stirring from the dream I was having.

"I'm bleeding. I'm fucking bleeding!" I hear Jasper's desperate pleas and scramble from the bed, losing my footing and landing in a heap on the floor, suffocated by the duvet. I untangle myself and rush to the door.

"Jasp, it's okay. Wake up, wake up." I hear Derek cooing as I make it to the entrance of Jasper's room. The lights are off and there's just a subtle blue glow highlighting them from the full moon casting its soft beam through the room. Derek sits beside Jasper's thrashing body. He reaches for him, bringing his head to his bare chest. It's heart wrenching to see the lines creasing Jasper's beautiful face as he struggles to overcome his nightmare.

"Derek, oh God, I was dreaming. It was a dream." The sweat from his body holds a shine, illuminating every dip in his sculpted torso, and his hair is soaking and stuck to his forehead. He grips onto Derek's arms like he needs the anchor to keep his nightmare from dragging him back in.

"Come on, shower. Let's wash the past off, Jasp." Der stands, wearing only a pair of lose fitting sleep pants; his frame is bigger than Jasper's and not as carved, but still toned, his abs defined and mouth-watering.

He holds his hand out for Jasper, who's still trying to calm his erratic breaths. Jasper slips his hand into Derek's, the duvet falling from him. *Oh God, he's naked.* The lust fires in Derek's eyes at the sight of him, but he doesn't seem surprised by the naked God in front of him. My eyes travel the length of him, my cheeks heating. My panties become wet from the arousal flooding them, the mild throb between my thighs makes me bite my lip hard to make me focus and bring me back to the fact that he's suffering.

They walk to his en suite, flicking the switch and lighting the room. I don't know whether to make my presence known, to offer to get him water or something, so I slip into his room and sit on the edge of his bed, debating. They've left the door half open and my line of vision is directly on them. I'm mesmerized by the affection I'm seeing. Derek turns the shower on, opening the door and gesturing for Jasper to step in. I watch in stunned silence, not even my breaths make a sound. I'm sure the world stopped, the clocks don't tick, the breeze becomes still—all in awe of the love, lust, and beauty in this bathroom.

Derek drops his trousers and steps inside with Jasper, his body folding over his back, his arms reaching under Jasper's arms to grip his chest. He rests his head against his shoulder and places kisses there. Jasper's head hangs, his arms resting against the shower wall, holding up his body as the water cascades over the two God-like creatures in the cubicle. He lifts his head, turning to find Derek's waiting lips. My stomach is on a rollercoaster. I feel light-headed as I watch them come together in an infusion of needy passion. Jasper turns in Derek's arms, reaching up and gripping his hair as their lips fuse and taste each other. I'm not experienced in the sexual department, but I know what I'm witnessing will probably never be topped as the most sensual sight I have, or ever will, witness. Their bodies rock against each other's, their erections touching and rubbing; they are both huge. I have seen a few, but never that size or perfection.

I stand and take a few steps closer, my eyes absorbing the wet orgasmic vision in front of them, my own ache growing with intensity and need.

My eyes feast on their display. Derek pulls away, pushing

Jasper until his back clashes with the tiled wall. Derek's mouth and hands cover every inch of Jasper's neck and torso in kisses and bites; their mixed groans echoing in the open space makes me need to hold my hand over my mouth to stop the moans escaping. Derek drops to his knees and my breathing hitches. *Oh God, oh God.*

"Take me in your mouth, Der. Suck my dick, make me forget."

My eyes tell my brain I'm being deceived and I'm expecting to wake in my bed at any second.

"Fuck, Der, all the way. That feels so fucking good."

I feel the coiling in my lower abdomen, the tingle up my spine, the hum in my veins spreading through my body. Jasper thrusts his hips forward into Derek's eager mouth, his erotic groans becoming more frequent as his hands tug on Derek's hair, pumping his hips faster.

"I'm going to come. Argh!" His body tenses, his face relaxing in pure ecstasy at his release. My legs fail me and I nearly fall to the floor.

A deep growl rips from Derek's chest. "You taste so fucking good, Jasp. Turn around."

My eyes spring wide and I know I've intruded more than should have. I rush back to my room, stripping off my bra and panties and slipping my fingers into my heated warm entrance, bringing myself to an overwhelming climax.

* * * * *

I wake to the warm glow of the sun heating my face. I roll onto my back with a yawn; the morning haze clears when the images of the night before rush in and I gasp, bolting upright and slipping from the bed. I look down at my naked body, my eyes closing.

"You're stunning." I jump at the sound of Jasper's voice. "Derek told me to bring you coffee." He stands from the chair at the other side of the bedroom and walks towards me. I should be embarrassed; I should grab the cover and hide my naked figure from his inquisitive gaze. His tongue swipes across his bottom lip as his eyes study everything I have on display. His body is mere inches from mine now. I feel the sexual pulse charging the air all around us; his hand comes forward and brushes my hair over my shoulder, uncovering my hardened nipple.

"God, you're so beautiful." His eyes lift from the newly discovered flesh to meet my own. His brows pinch as his eyelids drop slightly. "I wish so badly that she was you."

I'm confused by his statement and I'm lost in his gaze. He hands me the mug he's holding and I take it with a shaking grasp. I watch him shake his head and leave the room. I exhale in a rush and sit down on the bed until my heart settles and my legs gain back the strength to stand. I place the mug on the side table and slip into my clothes.

There's an air of nervous energy when I walk into the kitchen. Derek's eyes clash with mine and hold them hostage as I make my way to the sink to rinse my mug. Jasper reads an article on his laptop, his brow furrowed in concentration.

"Morning, Beauty. You sleep well?"

"Yes, thank you." The hitch in my voice makes me cough to try and cover it as my cheeks flame in a blush. He looks at me knowingly; my body has become rigid. *Did he know I was there watching them?* I break his gaze, adding my mug to the drainer.

"I need to go to work." He walks over and hands me a key. "Take the Lexus in the garage. You can drive that until you get your own."

"I can't …I don't…" I feel the press of his finger against my lips.

"You can. You need to be able to get around and the more time you spend driving, the more comfortable and confident you'll be doing it." He was right I know, but I just never liked driving. I witnessed a crash when I was young and it always stayed with me.

"Just take the car, Ky. It'll give us both peace of mind to know you can get around without risking public transport in seedy areas."

I roll my eyes at Jasper's *seedy* comment; they live in a mansion and anything outside it is a danger zone to them.

"Fine, thank you." I close my hand around the keys, and lean to place a kiss on Derek's cheek before leaving.

* * * * *

The smooth feel of the luxury car makes me more relaxed to drive. Its engine is just a quiet hum; the interior is refined and sleek. I know it's an expensive car and I feel a little self-conscious when I pull up at Twinkle Toes to see River arriving.

"Hey." She beams as I step out.

"Hey, Derek loaned me the car," I explain pointing over my shoulder to the golden champagne-coloured beauty.

"I love that car. He never drives it. I don't know why he even keeps it. At least someone is getting the use of it." She wraps her arm around my shoulder and squeezes. "How was the apartment hunt?"

I unlock the door and hold it open for her to pass. "Meh."

She chuckles. "That bad, huh? Well, you're welcome to stay with us as long as you need, you know that, right?"

I return her smile and nod. "Yes and thank you. I need to go change."

I walk to the back room where the lockers are. Dawn's inside slipping into a pair of leggings, and I notice a huge bruise on her thigh. It's the shape of a handprint. My gasp draws her attention and her eyes widen in a look of worry. She rushes to pull the tights up and shakes her head at me.

"Rough sex, Ky. Just because you're a prude doesn't mean we all are," she spits out, then puffs out a few breaths and steps over to me, putting her slim arms around me. "Fuck, that was really shitty. I'm sorry, I'm tired."

I embrace her hug and tell her it's fine. "We need to work with Amy from now until the end of the month. She has her audition for her placement," I say to change the subject.

"Okay."

I open the locker I rarely use to grab the change of clothes I shoved in here. I peer in and notice a folded piece of paper. Weird. Cautiously, I pull it out and unfold it.

He's really fond of you, "Beauty."
This makes it all the more rewarding.

My heart battles against my rib cage. I'm not sure what this even means or how long ago it was put there. They've caught the suspect who committed those assaults. What if those notes came from my ex after all, and this stalker case is just coincidence. *Beauty.* He used Derek's pet name for me. I shove the note back in the locker, change, and go to set up for the day.

Jasper

I can't believe Hannah triggered a nightmare. I had such a great night with Derek and Kyra, and then she texted to tell me she had a place she wants us to go see today. The suffocating choke hold came over me and I couldn't breathe. I tried to sleep, but the shit storm in my head wouldn't let me rest.

I must have passed out in the end because the next thing I knew, I was standing in front of Hannah, bleeding from the bullet wound left in my skin to remind me of what I lived through. She wasn't paying attention; she couldn't even see the blood.

I woke in Derek's arms like all the times before, and the relief was overwhelming. Being in his embrace felt too good: safe, warm, loved.

My heart is thawing, the steel grate I kept it in was left open and he seeped in and surrounded me in him. I think the affection for him must have always been there, somewhere in the depths of me, because I'm relieved to accept and welcome him.

It wasn't until after we left the shower that I remembered Kyra was sleeping across the hall. My gut twisted at the possibility of her seeing us, accepting us, joining us in there.

    Derek stayed in my room and set his alarm to wake early, so Kyra didn't see him leave my room. He made coffee and told me to go wake her. She was splayed across the bed. The naked, toned, and creamy skin of her back was on display, her hair fanned out in shiny waves; it looked like a small river of red wine. Her face was resting on a pillow, her lips slightly parted and tiny breaths escaping through the gap. I couldn't wake her, I just wanted to watch her in her peaceful slumber. When she rolled on to her back, yawning, her chest arching up, her fucking tits slipping free from the covers, she sat up, then stepped from the bed and I didn't have time to make my presence known. Seeing her naked, her smooth skin like satin wrapped around one of god's greatest achievement, was fucking awe inspiring; her tits sat high on her chest, a natural look that told me they would bounce when she was being made love to. *Made love to?* God, I was turning into Sammy, the love sick fuck.

    She was bare; her pussy as smooth as the rest of her, and fucking edible. I wanted to devour her. I could wake up next to her every day. Why couldn't she be standing there with her tummy swollen, my baby growing in there?

    I couldn't focus with both Kyra and Derek in the room, so when Kyra came down from her room, I tried to look busy. I was falling into the rabbit hole and it was scaring the shit out of me. When she left, Derek took me where I stood in a frenzied, intense way. I knew he felt the way I did for her, and having us both in the room tested all his restraint.

    Shortly after, I left to go meet Hannah at this house she was interested in. It was big, too big for two of us and a baby. How much room did the kid need? He would only be a foot long. The plush gardens and picket fences reminded me of

River's house. I was growing up and making a family; it didn't seem all that crazy anymore, accept for the person I was taking this leap with.

I wave back at Hannah, walking up the garden path to meet her. "This is Jesmond, our family's estate agent. He found this place for us and I think it's perfect."

I look Jesmond over; suit, combed hair with not a strand out of place, a Hollywood smile bought and paid for, a flash watch and a thing for Hannah. The fact that I don't give a shit that he's eye fucking her should have been enough for me to say *no way, I can't do this,* but the idea of letting my kid have a broken family is not acceptable to me. I can stop that from happening. Many other kids don't have a choice with who raises them, but mine will have their mom and me living together, loving and raising them.

"So, have you already looked around?" I ask, knowing this prick has already sold her the house; they just need my okay and signature.

"Well, I saw it yesterday, but wanted to show you."

I bite back the retort and let her show me around. The place is attractive, the warm tones of the décor have a family vibe, plus there are three extra bedrooms, one I can turn into a gym.

"So, what do you think?"

"It's lovely, big. Let me think it over."

She scowls at me; her hands defiantly placed on her hips "What's there to think about? It's perfect." The prick in the suit crosses his arms.

"I'm in business, Hannah. I need more than you telling me it's perfect before I sign anything. I'll look over everything and go from there."

"Fine." I watch her leave and follow behind her. "Don't

follow me, Jasp. I'm mad right now."

Fine by me.

I wave her off and head for home. I'm skipping work; I told Sammy I was busy house hunting all day, anyway.

I needed to go to the printers and pick up the photos River had managed to find for me of Mya. I went to her after the night Derek was at the cliff top, when he later told me he didn't even have a picture of her. I went to see River and nearly got caught by him when he came in the studio at the same time. River had gone to Mya's old high school and managed to get a year book that had quite a few photos of Mya inside.

She was stunning like her brother, and popular. It blows my mind to think that someone can impact someone else's self-esteem and mental state enough for them to end their life.

I took the book to a professional who could copy the pictures and crop out the others in the picture to make some perfect images of just Mya.

I go in to pay and collect them then, make my way to the studio to show them to River.

I'm hoping to avoid Kyra, but instead collide with her as I walk in.

"Oh, God!" She jumps, her hand coming up to her heart; she's pale, the green of her eyes swallowing the pupils. "You scared me."

I place a hand on her shoulder. "I only walked in, Ky. You look like you've seen a ghost. You okay?"

"Yeah." She chuckles, but it doesn't reach her eyes. "You just scared me is all. I need to go." She points to the dance room and strolls off.

"Hey, baby, what's up?" River greets me coming from her office.

"I wanted to show you the pictures. They're in the car."

She follows me out, and I open the boot and pull the main one from the protective wrap. Mya's eyes full of life look back at us from the picture.

"Oh God, Jasp, this is incredible. This will mean so much to him." She tears up and cries for twenty minutes non-stop into my shirt.

Derek

Last night while in the shower with Jasp, I was sure I saw a flash of red hair in my peripheral vision, but it was so quick I wasn't sure if it was a trick of the light.

Jasper was clearly having anxiety over things with Hannah, and they're the cause of his more frequent nightmares. I hate that he's stuck in this situation. I hate any time he spends with her. I have no claim to him yet I feel like he's mine. It's the same with Kyra. She's mine, too. I want to keep her safe. I want to support her with a home, but what I really want is for her to move in here with me and Jasper, but it can't happen.

I'm addicted, hooked on Jasper and everything he makes me feel emotionally and sexually. He's the best I have ever had and I can't even fathom giving that up.

I step into the lounge after getting home and showering. I halt, my heart seizes. Mya. A huge, unbelievably beautiful picture of her stunning smile stares back at me from over the fireplace. I can't take my eyes from her. There she is, my baby sister. God, she was so full of life then, her eyes alight with dreams, goals, passion.

"She was stunning, Der. I wanted you to have some pictures of her. She knew how much you loved her."

"How do you know that?" I answer, feeling Jasper behind me.

"Because it's there in your eyes. She would have seen it every time you looked at her."

"Where did you get these?" His hand goes into my hair and I relish his touch.

"River helped me track down Mya's year book."

God, he did this for me. He has no idea what he has just given me. Memories don't do her justice. I turn to face him and show him with every touch just how grateful I am to him.

* * * * *

All week Jasper has avoided Hannah. I saw the multiple missed calls from her on his cell. She's called the house, leaving messages, telling him she needs to see him, and yet he was in my arms in my bed every night for the last two weeks.

Kyra has come down with a cold, so I haven't seen her much, either. I'm in a love/lust Jasper bubble and I can't get enough.

The ringing of the doorbell makes Jasper stir next to me. I look at the clock. It's 7 a.m. What the hell?

"Grrrr, why are they hammering the doorbell like that?" Jasper grumbles.

I shift his weight away from me, garnering a moan from him and enticing me to stay right there. I pull a robe around my naked body and tread the stairs to the lobby. I can see Hannah pacing the doorstep from the camera above the door. I press the intercom.

"I heard the bell the first time."

Her scowl tightens her mouth, making her look older than her years. "I need to see Jasper."

I open the door and she barges past me, her heels *click-clacking* across the floor. Jasper is already making his way down the stairs and his eyes roll when they take in the morning visitor.

"I've been calling."

"I've been busy with work, sorry."

She scoffs at him and hands him a file. "I want the house, Jasp. We're either doing it together or I will do it alone."

He snatches the folder, looking sheepishly in my direction. "I'll have it sorted by the end of the day," he tells her.

She claps her hands together and leans in to kiss his cheek. "Thank you. We're going to be fine, Jasper. These are all teething problems."

Three weeks I've been inside him, every night. Fucking teething problems. This girl is insane.

"Mom wants to know when she can set the date. There's an opening at her country club, but we need to give them a definite by next week."

I'm fucking dizzy right now; vertigo is making the room spin.

"I'll call you later and maybe we can have dinner this week."

I hear him speaking, but it's in slow motion. I knew this was all going to have to end, but I've been living in the bubble where I didn't think about the when and why, and every other reason I shouldn't be completely in love with him.

I hear her clanking heels as she passes me and slams the door behind her.

"She wants to buy a house."

I can't say anything. Nothing for him has changed and I know to him this is sexual and nothing more. "Come back to bed, Jasp."

His eyes flash with surprise which quickly turns to heat. If this is all it is to him, then I'll give him the best sex of his life.

* * * * *

Three hours in every position. I'm aching in all the right places and still it isn't enough. Kyra had called and asked me to meet her at River's. I haven't told her yet that I've found her a property and laid down the first years rent. I know she's a proud woman, but I need to know she's living somewhere safe and clean and worthy of her.

I pull up and toot the horn. Kyra comes out of the studio looking rosy cheeked from the workout the dancing gave her.

"Hey," she says, leaning into kiss my cheek.

My lips capture hers on impulse; her soft, petite lips pucker, caressing mine before moving back. "Hey," I reply with a grin. "I have somewhere I want to take you."

Her smile is hypnotic. "Where?"

"I'll show you."

We stand in the middle of her new lounge; the cream walls give the place a fresh look. I had movers completely fill it with brand new furnishings.

A tear leaks to her cheek. "Beauty, what's wrong?" The pad of my thumb captures her stray tear.

"It's just so nice. I can't afford it and can't let you just pay my rent, Derek."

I cup her cheek, and she burrows into my hand, firing the alpha male tendencies in me. "I know the realtors and got a cracking deal, Ky. It's the same as you're paying now."

Her eyes grow big and her mouth pops open. She looks around. "Really?"

I pull her into me and give her a gentle squeeze. I know this will be the only way she'll accept the place.

"Thank you," she whispers against my chest.

"What did you want to talk about?"

She looks conflicted, her brow pinching. She looks to her purse, then back at me. "Nothing, it was nothing. I just missed spending time with you is all."

"Well, how about we go get your stuff, move you in here, and have dinner?"

"Sure."

Kyra

He seems so happy; how can I tell him I received another note? He'll go into full on protective detective. I can't believe this beautiful place he got for me. I'm not worried, the note is similar to the first ones I got and nothing else is happening. Derek is keeping me updated via text about the condition of the suspect; he's still in a coma, so I know this just has to be my ex playing games and I won't let him turn everyone's lives upside down.

"I just need to get my things from River's. I can do my place another time."

I pack away my things and feel a little sad to be leaving them. I've grown really close to Mikey and I'll miss him. His behaviour has settled remarkably and this is just a beautiful atmosphere to be in.

We wait for River to bring Mikey home from school, so I can say goodbye to him properly and explain where I'm moving to. He cries, which in turn makes me cry, which then makes River cry. Der doesn't know who to hug first.

"You okay?" Derek asks, taking my last bag inside the new place.

I smile and follow him in. "I'm fine. I'm not sure what we're going to eat though. I need to buy groceries."

"I text Jasper to bring something over after he's done …with paperwork."

I watch the pain cross his face and hear the falter in his voice. "What's going on?"

"What do you mean?"

"I mean, what's he really doing?"

He breathes hard and scrubs his hands down his face. The strain is evident in his features. "He's buying a house for him and Hannah."

My head swims and my stomach curdles as the hot tears gather, then flood to my face. I'm mortified by my reaction. It's the knowing he doesn't want to be with her that feels so final. It was seeing the connection him and Derek share that is more than any I have ever seen outside the passion Sammy has for River. It's the knowing I'll never fulfil that yearning I have for him.

I try to turn from Derek's penetrating gaze, but he captures my chin and forces me to look at him. "I know how you feel about him."

I fight the tears from coming and sniffle, "And I know how you feel about him, Derek. Worst of all, I know how little she feels for him and it hurts knowing she gets him."

He pulls me into his chest, his warm, big hands soothing me as they rub gentle circles on my back. "Go wash your face so he doesn't see you've been crying. He'll be here soon."

I go to the bathroom and wash up, then change into some fresh clothes and brush my hair loose. I need to get over these feelings I have for him and move forward. I want more from Derek. I knew he was in love with Jasper, but maybe he can love us both, and we can heal each other when Jasper moves on.

Derek

Dinner was rushed and felt a little uncomfortable; as soon as Ky cleared the plates, I was putting my coat on.

I kiss Kyra on the lips and fight back the groan as Jasper leans in, brushing his body against mine and placing a kiss just below her ear. God, I'm greedy and I want them both. I wait for her to lock the door before I make my way to my place. Jasper had gone to the studio to collect the Lexus and drove it here, so she'll have transport in the morning. The drive home is done in a tense stand-off. I know he's signed the papers to move in with Hannah and it cuts me deep. I don't want him to move out; the dark hole is opening up inside me again. I already miss him before the goodbye.

I follow Jasper into the lobby; he empties his pockets on the console table. "Don't do this, Jasp."

He bows his head like he knew this was coming. "I'm going to shower, Der."

I don't follow him, even though every inch of my sexual desire is screaming at me to. I go to the bar and pour myself a drink; it warms my stomach as it hits and spreads through my body. I can't see how I can go on living without him now I know what it's like to have him. Before, it was different. I didn't think there was a possibility of ever having him, but now I have? God, how can I live watching him with her?

I drown my sorrows and try to wash it all away, but it just grows with urgency.

"Der, you smell like a brewery. Come to bed."

I push my glass away and swipe the near empty bottle, then make my way to my room. He's waiting for me and the tightening in my chest is almost unbearable. "Don't leave me for her, Jasp." I know I'm drunk, my words slur his name. I feel weak, helpless, my brain raging war with itself on reasons why I need him, and he shouldn't be with her to the fact that I know it's more complicated than me just wanting to keep him.

"Der, you knew this was happening. I can't let my kid wake up in a house I don't live in."

"Then share custody."

Jasper shakes his head. "You're drunk."

I grab his wrist and place his hand over my heart that's beating a mile a minute. "Don't act like you don't know how I feel, Jasper. This has always been more than just sex to me."

His face softens as his hand grasps the nape of my neck. "This is more to me, too. But you know I have to leave. You know I have to marry her."

I feel my insides shatter. How could I let myself get in this deep? I look him over and think of the life he'll live with her, with our affection. The ache is so powerful it's almost a being all on its own. I mimic his hold, my hand gripping tight to the nape of his neck.

I look him in the eye and lay all my feelings there at his feet like a bleeding wound draining the life from me. It's the most vulnerable and heart-felt I've ever allowed myself to be. "Keep me… keep me in your mind with the memories we shared. Keep me in your heart with each erratic beat you feel when I look at you. Keep me in the essence of your soul with the part of mine you own there. Keep me imprinted on your skin with the memories of my touch. Keep me on your lips with the thoughts of when mine would brush against yours. Those memories and thoughts are ours. Mine and yours to keep forever, to visit when the ache builds, when the pain becomes unbearable, when you reach over the bed and feel the space where my body used to lay, when you wish it was my voice, my touch, my love, my scent engulfing you, living you, breathing you every day."

I clash my lips to his, so he can't respond. There's nothing more he can say. I know it's over and this is my goodbye.

* * * * *

I leave the bedroom before he wakes, shower, and change, then make my way down the stairs. Hans called, telling me the suspect is awake. I need to question him and close this case.

I grab my keys and notice a note with Jasper's things. The detective, nosey side of me wins out and I open it. My keys drop on the floor with a clank as I read the words.

He will pay, Beauty, and you're the cost.

I race up the stairs. "Jasp wake up!" I shake him.

"What the fuck, Der? Come back to bed. Someone's waking up." He grins, fisting his cock. This has got to be the first time mine doesn't salute him.

"Where did this come from?" I hold up the note and his

brow furrows as he snatches it from my hand.

"Where did you get this?" he asks.

"With your keys. You put it on the console table when you came in."

He sits up, alert. "It was on the window wipers of the Lexus. That girl who works there, Dawn was outside and I assumed she was putting out leaflets."

He stands and pulls on his jeans that were thrown on the floor. "Call Kyra."

My heart stops. Oh God, I left her alone. I pull my cell out and call her number. My life span shortens with every unanswered ring.

"Hello…Derek?" Her groggy voice hums down the line.

I collapse to the bed, relieved. "You okay, Beauty?"

I hear her moving around. "I'm fine. What's this about? Is it about the Jasper thing?"

I look up at him, concern etched on his face. "No, listen, Ky. I don't want you to leave the apartment okay? I'm sending Jasper over until I'm free; don't question me on this, just say okay, please."

"Okay," she agrees.

I end the call. "You need to go stay with her until I can get there."

"On my way."

* * * * *

Hans meets me outside as I get to the hospital.

"It's not him." Those are his first words as he approaches me. "He was approached in a bar. This guy fitting the same description as the suspects bought him drinks all day, then handed him the keys to his car."

A flush of ice cold dread washes through my veins. "I need you to run everything on Evan again."

"Sure thing."

I call Sammy to warn him to stick close with River, and I spend the day chasing dead ends. I'm left frustrated, angry. Why hadn't he struck when we believed the suspect was caught? *Because it's personal and he wants me to feel this, the anxiety, anticipating his next move.*

I pack up and make my way to Kyra's

Kyra

It was hard being around Jasper; his whole personality cloaked the air and I was drowning in him when he took Hannah's call and agreed on a date for their wedding. Time ceased to exist. It stopped with my heart. Three weeks from now he'll be married. I need to squash the feelings that have blossomed and expanded with rapid growth.

"Derek's outside, Ky. I need to go sort some things with Hannah. I can come back later if you want?"

"No, do your thing. We'll be fine."

He smiles and kisses me, leaving a burning crater in its wake traveling from the kiss to every part of me. My nerves eat away at me while I wait for Derek to appear. When he does, he looks tired and miserable.

"Why didn't you tell me about these notes?" He holds up the one I had given to Jasper earlier. I drop my head.

"I'm sorry, I just thought it was my ex being a douche. I didn't want to ruin your thing with Jasp, you seemed happy and…"

He stops me, putting a hand over my mouth. The look he's giving me is of awe. "You saw us."

I fight the blush, but it ignites my skin. I walk away from him into my room, embarrassed to admit I had watched them. He follows me.

"You saw us," he repeats.

"Yes, but Derek, he is going to marry her. Neither of us can keep him. He set the date. Three weeks from now, he'll marry her."

"I know I can't keep him. I said goodbye to him last night. It's over."

I look up at him and see the painful truth. I know how he feels. I can't have Jasper and a part of me will mourn that, but the part that has fallen for Derek just wants him to make me his.

"I want to move forward. I want to be something more. I want *us* to be more. I've never felt this way before. I have to be with you. Own me, Derek, make me yours."

I suck air into my lungs, trying to feel what I just released in my confession.

I slip the straps from my shoulders and my dress puddles at my feet, leaving me bare to his warm gaze. My ragged breaths lift my breasts with each intake.

"You are mine, Kyra. We own each other now."

He steps closer to me, his breath blowing over my hair, his big hands stroking down my arms. "You're exquisite, *my beauty*, so perfect."

His lips press to my neck, whispering across the sensitive skin there. "Lay on the bed."

I comply, lying down across the satin sheet. He pulls the knot from his tie, slipping it from him. His belt follows; the clunk makes my body jerk with anticipation as it hits the floor. I watch as he slowly unbuttons his shirt, his eyes never leaving me. I'm so nervous, but also so ready to experience this, and after Jasper told me that he'll be marrying Hannah, I realised I could have wasted myself by giving myself to him. Yet here stood Derek in all his manly perfection looking down at me like I'm the only women he has ever desired. His lust-filled gaze has my heart beating wildly in my chest; lightning bugs have taken flight in my stomach, making my skin hum with sensitivity.

His shirt falls away and he steps closer, his knees skimming the bed. His hands rest on my knees, and he gently pulls them apart. My hot, wet need for him evidently on display for his greedy eyes. "You are so divine."

My teeth bite down hard down on my lip as I watch him remove his trousers. "Oh God," I breathe before I can stop myself. His huge erection, smooth and glistening on the tip, stands heavy up his stomach.

I gulp down the nerves and watch in fascination as he gets to his knees, wraps his arms around my calves and pulls me down the bed. His hot breath kisses my dampened lips before I feel his warm tongue swipe out. My head falls back as little shocks of pleasure sing through my body.

"Mmmm, you taste pure. Fucking divine, Beauty."

His mouth devours me—sucking, licking, kissing. I feel like I could take flight on the high I'm feeling. I've never felt anything this cathartic in my twenty-three years. My muscles tense, and an explosion of pleasure erupts inside me.

"God, Beauty, that's it. Let go."

"Oh, God Derek! Oh, God." The stars finally clear from my eyes and Derek's intense gaze replaces it, his heavy frame resting over me. I feel the brush of his cock and a whimper escapes my mouth.

"You sure about this, Beauty? I can wait."

"No, I want you. I'm yours. Claim me, Derek."

The primal growl that leaves him makes me shiver. I've

never felt more wanted. I feel the pressure as he pushes his cock inside me; it's surreal and wonderful all at once. The sting of him taking my virginity lasts only seconds before the fullness makes my body take flight. Every gentle stroke of his cock heightens me to new pleasures; the power of his body thrusting into mine makes me want to weep. He is so strong and beautiful; my lips feather kisses over his chest, up his neck until I claim his mouth with mine, his tongue dancing with mine as he continues to thrust into me. My body trembles and tightens as my orgasm takes control of my body, squeezing Derek's release from him.

He collapses over me, rolling to the side and pulling me into his chest. "You're mine now, Kyra."

And I am.

Derek

It was different waking up to the sweet scent of Kyra instead of the earthy tones of Jasper. Her hair fans across my chest, her breasts pushing into my torso. She is a goddess and I have her in my arms. There's no way I'm letting her go.

I know I have to face Jasper, and I locked all those feelings away. I owe it to Kyra to give her all of me and I want to for the first time in my life. I want to give myself to a woman.

The worry over Evan is like a dark shadow hovering over me, though. I need to find him. Jasper mentioned Dawn putting the note on the car. I had to start somewhere.

I gently slip from underneath her, hurrying to get dressed. I call Hans and tell him to send a patrol car over here to stake the place while I'm out.

"Where are you going?" Her sleep infused voice filters through the air as her sleepy form stretches out.

"I need to follow up on a lead. I have an officer outside."

She sits up. The covers bunched at her waist exposing her upper body. My cock stiffens at the beauty on display. "That's not needed, Der. He hasn't done anything other than send the notes."

"That's all it was before he attacked and assaulted the other girls, too. This is personal and I'll be damned if I don't take every precaution to keep you from harm. Pack a bag, you're moving in with me."

Her jaw drops. "I just moved in here."

"Kyra, pack a bag. You're mine now, which means you belong with me."

A smile plays on her lips. "Okay."

"Good."

Jasper

I agreed on a date. It's set. No Kyra, no Derek, just Hannah and our kid. Life has really played a sick joke on me; the tide is coming in fast and I can't swim. Everything Derek told me last night, not waking up to him or having him love me, uncoiled the feeling I was trying to deny from him and myself. I'm in love with him; I crave him and want to be in his breathing space all the time. Instead, I'm standing in Hannah's apartment. Why can't she be Kyra? For Kyra, I could have put aside all the things I feel for Derek. I could have just had her, she would be enough.

"Here."

I take what she offers, looking at the black and white image. I've seen these before with River; it's a scan picture.

"When did you have this done?"

"Yesterday. My mom came with me."

"Why the fuck didn't you ask me to come?"

"Because you were doing stuff with that family of yours that you don't want me to be a part of."

"That's bullshit, Hannah, and you know it."

She cocks her overplucked eyebrow, and dammit, the

bitch is right.

"Fine. Well, River is cooking tonight, so come for dinner," I challenge her. She can say I don't want her to be a part of them all she liked; the truth is, she doesn't want to mix with them and hates how close we all are.

"Fine, I will."

"Good. See you tonight."

* * * * *

Derek didn't come home last night. I knew he was worried and staying with Kyra, but he hadn't replied to my texts and I'm worried when I phone Kyra.

She sounds hesitant. "He stayed here and left for work about an hour ago."

"Who's with you, then?"

"A patrol car is outside."

"You okay?"

She breathes heavy down the line. "Yeah, I'm good. Jasp, I need to shower." She's trying to get me off the line.

"Okay, talk soon."

I end the call and go to see River to let her know Hannah will be joining us for dinner.

Mikey is running round the yard when I get there. I kick his new ball towards him and his face lights up as he races to it. He seems content, and after everything, it's good to see.

"Hey, baby," River greets me.

"Hey, baby," Sammy mocks, winking at me.

"Your hair looks good, River."

She touches her new haircut. "Thank you. Sammy is taking me out tonight, so dinner's tomorrow night. Did Sammy call you?"

I glare in his direction. "No."

He lifts his hand in a "don't shoot me" pose. "You've been acting like an asshole and ignoring my calls, and I can tell you if you don't answer check your voicemail before you act hard done by."

He's right, I have been. I was worried he would know everything that was happening with me from just the look on my face.

"So, do I get the boy tonight?"

River fidgets. "Actually, I just asked Ky. I didn't know if you were busy with Hannah. Kyra said you set the date. Which is something that would have been nice to hear from you."

"I'm sorry, it's all happening so fast. Oh, here," I reach in my pocket and pull the scan photo out. I don't know how I feel about it. I've come around to the idea of having a kid; I don't have a choice, so it's something I just accepted. But seeing the image in front of me, I just can't decipher what I'm feeling.

"When did you go have this?"

"I didn't. She went with her mom."

A look of wonder lights up her face, then clouds and her brow pinches. "Jasp, how far along is she?"

"Not far. She's already rounding in her tummy though, and having image issues about it. Fuck, you women don't realise you're beautiful when pregnant and it doesn't matter how round you get."

I stroke her tummy. She takes my hand in hers. "This is a twenty week scan, Jasp. Look at these numbers down the side, it tells you the estimated gestation."

I look at the technical numbers printed down the side of the scan photo. "They must have given her the wrong picture."

She looks over at Sammy, then back to me.

He strides over, taking the picture. "Her name is printed

on it. She's with your doctor," Sammy tells River.

"We should go there. The receptionist has a thing for me; we can get her to show us her file."

River snorts. "She won't show you her file, Sammy, with that smile or not."

"Car, Jasp. We're getting this shit sorted right now."

I walk with him like a zombie. Why would she lie? Why would she want me to father a kid that wasn't mine, or to marry her? She doesn't even like me. She likes my dick and that's all. It doesn't make sense.

Sammy was right; the receptionist's eyes nearly fall out of her head when he walks in. She fluffs her hair in an attempt to make it look better. It's a mess, but I put on my panty-dropping smile that has bagged me many one night stands, and go in for the kill. Sammy leans over the counter with a grin I've seen him use to conquer any woman he used it on.

"Hey, sweetheart. So, my girl," I shrug my shoulders when her smile slips slightly. "My soon-to-be ex girl, gave me this." I hand her the scan, her smile faltering again. "I'm told that's an eighteen week scan and she can't possibly be that far along. I was just wondering if you can get her up on your computer and confirm this?"

She nibbles on a pen, her eyes darting between Sammy and me, then around the room. "I can't do that. I'm sorry, all patient files are confidential."

Sammy skims up, moving me out the way. He reaches out, clasping her hand, then checks her name tag and tilts his head to the side. "Kelly, you seem like a decent girl. Beautiful, honest?" Her eyes cast over with a dreamy fixated stare. "You wouldn't trick a guy into marriage with a pregnancy that's not his, right?"

Her mouth drops open and she shakes her head. "He has

his wedding in three weeks and if she's lying about this, he'll be stuck in a marriage he doesn't want to be in with a lying bitch who's carrying someone else's child."

She looks around the room again, then opens a drawer and puts a set of keys on the desk. "I can't show you the files we keep on computer or the printed files we keep in the file case alphabetised by last name as it's confidential. Did you say the coffee machine was jammed? I can come help you with that." She winks at Sammy.

"Yes please, I need my coffee; it gives me much needed energy. I like to keep my stamina up," he drawls.

I wait for her to come around the desk, then go to work on the filing cabinet. It doesn't take long to find the key and her folder. There are appointments for the pregnancy dating back to just after we met. Fuck, she was already a couple months pregnant. That fucking bitch. This kid isn't mine. Why the fuck would she want me?

I notice a photocopy machine; I print off a copy, then put the file back and leave the keys on her desk.

Kelly's giggling at something Sammy says when I locate them at the coffee machine in the back of the room. "Let's go. Kelly was it? You're a sweetheart, thank you." She blushes and waves as Sammy and I leave.

"Well?"

I hand him the printed copy. "She's a fucking liar."

"Son of a bitch. Why the fuck would she lie?"

"Let's go ask her."

Sammy follows me inside the apartment where Hannah is drinking a cup of coffee. I asked her not to drink it while pregnant. She looks up at us, surprised to see me and Sammy, who has never set foot in her place until now.

I throw the copy down on the table. "Why the fuck

would you lie about the baby being mine?"

Panic, then indifference passes across her face. She picks up the paper and rolls her eyes. "Who'd you fuck to get this, the receptionist?" she sneers.

"Answer the fucking QUESTION!" I roar.

"Why is he here?" She flicks her chin up at Sammy. He steps around me, leans his hands on the table and gets near her face.

"Because I'm his brother, bitch, and you're lying about his kid."

She scowls and stands, her hands on her hips with a stance of defiance. She narrows her eyes at me, then rolls them. "Fine, you're right. It's not yours." She release a heavy breath, then slumps back down in her chair. "I'm sorry, I panicked. He's married… and my dad's best friend."

"You mean Dr. Blake?" He is old as fuck. He has kids the same age as her.

Her hands go to her temples, rubbing in small circles. "I know you won't understand, but I love him, Jasper. He won't leave his wife. I didn't know I was pregnant when I slept with you. I did it to punish him for not leaving her. I was willing to risk losing my parents to be with him. When I found out and told him, he lost it, and told me that we had to keep it a secret. I told him about you and he said I should raise the baby as yours because my mom would disown me if I wasn't going to marry and settle down with the father."

I can't believe what I'm hearing from her; ruining my life because some cheating, fucking pervert didn't want the shit to hit the fan.

"You know what she's like and I panicked. I didn't want to be a single parent and watch him from the side lines."

"So fuck what was best for Jasper then, you conniving

bitch!" Sammy grates out.

"Get the fuck out of my apartment, you have no idea what I'm going through!" she shouts.

"This is fucked up, Hannah. Who were you with when you said you were picking wedding dresses with your mom?"

Guilt flashes in her eyes, but it's fleeting. "Him. He had a conference."

"So you're still fucking him? Why the condoms?"

She stands again, snarling at me. "Because you're a fucking slut. I know you're fucking that Derek and Kyra. I'm not stupid. You reeked of sex when I came round that morning, both of you naked under a robe. She was probably passed out in the bed."

I nearly spew on her table as my guts clench. Why would she say that shit in front of Sammy? I can't get words out. I chance a glimpse at Sammy, but he's just sneering at her.

"Oh don't look like a deer in the headlights, Jasper, everyone can see it. Sammy knows." She scoffs. "Derek looks at you like a starving puppy. It's pathetic, and her, she's…"

"STOP FUCKING TALKING! This is done."

"I'm keeping the house."

"Like fuck are you. You are seriously deluded. Come on, Sammy."

Sammy takes the keys from me and drives. "You got a lucky escape today."

I can't look at him. I'm waiting for him to bring up what she said about Derek and I feel nauseated.

"Jasp, you're like a brother to me. Nothing anyone says or anything you do will ever change that. I don't care where you put your dick; I just want you to find the happiness I have with River. I love you and want that for you."

I feel like a woman. My emotions are all over the place

and I swallow back the lump in my throat. I needed to hear him tell me that so badly. "Thanks and I think I have." My voice sounds hoarse from the emotion I'm fighting. I'm trying to keep it together. A world of possibilities just opened up for me.

"You coming back to my place?"

"No, I want to go home and clear my head."

"Fair enough."

Derek

I locate Dawn's address and find her with a black eye. The sight coils my stomach.

"Who did this Dawn?" She leaves the door open for me to follow her inside.

"It's nothing. Why are you here?" Her voice wavers, and her hands hold a tremble.

"I need to know why you put this on Kyra's car window." I hold up the note, her teeth come out to worry her lip.

"I don't know what you're talking about." A tear brings to light her betrayal and guilt.

"It's okay. I can keep you safe. I just need to know who and where, Dawn. Let me help you. Let me help Kyra."

"I'm so sorry. He threatened me! He made me leave her the notes." She's soon crying and I want to offer her comfort, so I place a hand on her shoulder.

"Where is he now?"

Her mascara streaks her face. Her blue eyes shine from the unshed tears. She's a real pretty woman and can do a million times better than any asshole who would take his fists to her.

"He's a lorry driver, and he's away right now. He won't be back until next week."

"License plate? What name is he using?"

"I don't know the plates, but his name is Evan Mills." His name makes me want to vomit and kill all in the same breath.

I call all the truck companies in the state and come up empty. He's a sly snake, slithering his way through all my resources. I have nothing to go on. All I can do is a wait for him to mess up or strike. The thought is grinding me down.

River had called, telling me she asked Kyra to babysit tonight so I arranged a squad car to stake out Sammy and River's place. I need to go tell Jasper about the development with Kyra and me. I'm not looking forward to this. I know it'll hurt to see him, but I need to remember this is Jasper. He doesn't do love; he fucks and he's good at it.

My phone rings and I'm surprised to see it's River again. "What's up?"

"Sammy just got back from dropping Jasper back at your house. Hannah was lying about the baby. It isn't his."

I'm in shock; it's the only explanation for me dropping the phone and emptying my stomach all over the floor. There's just too much going on; I had taken Kyra's virginity last night under the impression neither of us could be with Jasper, so we deserve to be happy with each other, and now everything has changed for him on a huge scale. I can't be with him now. I gave myself to Beauty and she gave herself to me. I can't hurt her like that; the very idea of hurting her twists my insides.

I pick up my phone. "Sorry, Riv. So what's happening?"

"The wedding and everything is off. He got a lucky escape. Now he can be with someone he loves, Der."

"I have to go." I end the call and spend an hour just driving around before I man up and do what I need to do.

* * * * *

I find Jasper in his room when I get home. I can't pussyfoot. I need to just do this.

"Seems you're off the hook, then?"

I don't feel the relief like I thought I would. I think it's ironic. I went to tell him Kyra and I are an official couple now, and just like that, everything changed and it's too late to take back the night I had with her. I wouldn't ever want to. I do love her, but my head and heart are in turmoil over this.

He's wearing jeans and no shirt; his body is so perfect I want to trace every dip with my tongue, but that wouldn't be fair to Kyra. I couldn't hurt her after she gave me something so precious.

He stands up, giving me a full view of his perfection, then strides towards me, stopping a couple of feet from me. "I can't believe her. I feel so relieved and then guilty for feeling that way because even though she was lying, I still feel like I lost something, you know? I had talked myself round to the idea of having a kid."

I want to wrap my hands around Hannah's throat and tighten, which is a first for me. "She's a bitch. You don't want that for your kid. This is an escape, so think of it as one," I tell him. He smiles up at me and I feel the need to hold him. Fuck, this is going to be so hard.

"Listen, Jasp, I know this is shitty timing, but Kyra and me… we're official now. I asked her to move in."

His smile drops. I watch his pulse flicker rapidly in his throat as his jaw twitches. "So what does that mean for us?"

I clear my face of all emotion. I don't want him to see how much I care for him because this is Jasper and Jasper is only in this for the thrill. I step back. "There is no us. We fucked, now we won't, and you can go back to fucking whatever little slut opens her legs for you."

I feel like an asshole. His face has gone pale. His chest heaves and his eyes have glassed over. What the hell? I just want to hold him.

Jasper

"I might be into sex with easy women and maybe I'm too closed off to let people in when it comes to love and shit. My dad lost my mom and he fucking loved her with every fibre of his soul. It destroyed him when she died. I was a baby, but I felt the sorrow. It lived with us! I still have fucking feelings. Derek! I feel just like you do, I hurt just like you, and I'm hurting right now. How can you just shrug me off like I'm nothing to you? A fuck? Are you serious right now? I can't believe this. I didn't WANT TO FEEL THIS!" I shout at him. My body feels physical pain, my chest constricting, like a wormhole had opened up inside my stomach, sucking my soul through it.

I can't believe what he just said. He opened my eyes to something I'd only ever fantasised about and then made me feel something for him. I don't do feelings, but he crawled inside, changing me, for what? To drop me like I'm nothing? Fuck, my body is trembling, I can't control it. How can my heart physically hurt? It feels like he's closed a fist around it and liquefied it in his palm.

Oh God, this is Karma. I can't believe I fell; it's just as painful as I thought it would be. It's gut wrenching, heart twisting. I want to cry right now. I want to pour every ounce of whatever the fuck this is I'm feeling and cry it out. It's poison. It corrupts my mind, telling me I can have something I fucking can't.

"I want to go back and never take that step if this is what I feel in the end. I can't take it. I'm not as strong as you," I mumble. I look up into his brown eyes; I see nothing of the Derek who has been there for the last month. He's stone faced. "You know what makes this twice as bad? Kyra. Derek, why her? You knew I had a thing for her. Is this some kind of punishment? Did I fucking wrong you?"

He steps forward all commanding, dripping with authority. He grabs the back of my head, tugging on my hair. I can't fucking help it, I get hard. "You just wanted to fuck Kyra. She deserves more than that. She's not like the sluts you fuck. She was fucking pure."

"Was?" I choke out.

He releases me from his hold and shoves me back. "Stop acting like a fucking brat just because you're not getting your own way, Jasper."

I don't understand any of this. I can't deal with it. Fuck him, fuck her, fuck everyone. I stride to my dresser, pull a t-shirt out and slip it over my head. I don't even look at him when I leave.

I gave him something I hadn't given anyone before. I gave him me, my heart, my passion, my fucking soul. I gave them both a part of me and here I am with nothing. A burned out fire, that's all I am to him.

I need them out. I need to lock that door to my heart and bury the key in concrete. I need to find someone to lose myself in.

* * * * *

Sweat clings to the air; the dark scent cloaks my clothing. The intense music has a heavy beat just like my heart, beating so fucking loud and hopelessly people can feel it in and around them like an entity.

I feel myself drowning in flashes of Derek with Kyra, laughing at me. Why would he do this? I opened up to him, trusted him, and thought we were sharing something special. I'm lost, floating with no direction in choppy waters. He's a fraud. He made me believe I was more and maybe worthy of falling for. He made me rethink my whole life. I feel like I'm out in a blizzard—cold and lonely, looking in through a window at love and happiness that will never be mine.

I should never have opened my heart. This is why I fuck and don't fall in love, to avoid this self-hating misery.

I know I was going to marry Hannah before I found out she's a lying whore. But it doesn't mean I don't feel these feelings for Derek. He opened my whole world up. I'm a stranger to these emotions; I need to get back to who I was before them, before him. I need to go back to what I'm used to. I need to forget, drown out and wash away what happened and never think of it again.

I look around the club I'd been told about by an old friend from back home. His brother owns a sex club and has branched out. So here I am, watching people grind against each other on the dance floor while some fuck in booths where people can watch. There are private rooms for members, but I don't want to fuck here. I need to do it at my place to wipe out whatever I felt with Derek there. I make eye contact with a little red head who's been eyeing me since I walked in. She's wearing full leathers and trying to look intimidating, but she just looks stupid and her red hair is not something I can get on board with; too much like Kyra's.

I want a blonde. My eyes dart around the club and lock with a broad blonde-haired guy. His hair is long, but pulled back in a tie. He has a presence that emanates dominance.

I tear my eyes from his and look around the people hovering near him; they're all watching him with longing. He stands up and I feel my heartbeat stampede in my chest. He's wearing black jeans, a black tee with a black leather jacket and motorcycle boots. He must stand around six foot six. Fuck, before Derek I had never felt any lust for a male before. I had entertained the idea maybe in a threesome, but never ever went there until Derek.

Before he reached me, my view was interrupted by a black leather waist. My eyes travelled the valley of her fake tits, then up her throat to her face.

"Hey, pretty boy. You want to play?" God, her voice is weak and whiny.

"Not with you he doesn't. Stop playing dress up, Ruby. You give this club a bad name."

She scurries off with her eyes downcast. His voice is deep and masculine. He towers over me, studying my face before he grasps the front of my shirt, guiding me to rise. He leans down to my ear. "We staying or leaving? Either way, I'm fucking you."

Holy shit, I'm thankful for the bottle of Jack I drank in my car, giving me the courage to come in here to do this. I needed it and this guy has my blood sizzling in my veins at the possibility I could use him to wipe Derek's memories and touch out.

"Leaving," I mumble.

He walks to the exit. "My truck's over here." His tone leaves no room for argument, so I climb in. We don't speak; the air is electrified with anticipation. I type the area code into his GPS and let the sexual tension build all the way home.

He seems indifferent by the mansion; clearly money isn't something he cares about. I open the door. There's no movement downstairs. I stride up the stairs with him behind me, push my bedroom door open and stand in the centre. My heart races.

"Music?" He breathes down my neck with his body pushing against my back. My breath comes out choppy as I point to the sound system. He shrugs his jacket off, throwing it on a chair in the corner of the room, then reaches for the collar of his t-shirt, pulling it with ease over his head, the muscles in his back flex with the movement.

I follow suit, ridding myself of my t-shirt just as a knock comes at the door. I turn towards it as Jared Leto croons from the speakers. I open the door and come face to face with Derek standing in the dim light of the hallway.

"Can we talk?" he asks.

I smirk as the half-naked man steps up behind me; he reaches around my waist and tugs at my fly, popping the buttons. "He's busy," he growls over my shoulder and shuts the door in Derek's face.

"Is he why you're doing this?" The fucker was perceptive.

"Does it matter?" I slur.

He studies me and I feel angry at his scrutiny. He came here to fuck a stranger, so what did he care if it was a revenge fuck or a forget fuck? I can't take it; the alcohol is only amplifying the emotional dilemma I'm having. I slide down the door, my knees coming up to my chest.

I am a mess. How can this be me? I want to kick my own ass.

The music volume increases, drawing my attention to this guy. "Let's lay on the bed, you're wasted."

I am. I let him help me up and into the bed. My head feels heavy as it makes contact with the pillow. Darkness claims me.

Derek

A mind prison, that's all I can describe it as. My fucking mind is locked in Jasper's room. My stomach has abandoned me down the john. My heart is a slow thump; it's giving up. I can't cope with the knowledge that he's in there being fucked by some guy. He is mine, but he's not.

The music vibrates his walls and I'm grateful I can't hear them. My mind is already in there, seeing them together. The dominant male in me wants to smash the door down and put a bullet in this joker's head, but I risk hurting and losing Kyra now. It's a wreck, and the destruction is devastating.

All night that album plays, that guy's voice will forever haunt me.

I make the coffee, gripping the pot in a vice hold, so I don't beat this Chris Hemsworth-looking guy who just entered my kitchen to death with it.

"We just slept. I shouldn't give a shit, but I know what he's feeling and you should know he just passed out and we slept." He walks away.

I pour Jasper a mug and take it to him. His room has its usual scent of Jasper's body products. He's lying out cold on the bed, his jeans open and his arm flung over his eyes. I have to fight the need to pin him to me and thank him for being too drunk to destroy everything we did. I didn't just fuck him. I made love to him. I love him.

I leave the coffee on the bedside table and go to work.

* * * * *

The leads are still coming up as dead ends. The suspect in the hospital story was confirmed by the bar keeper who gave us a description of Evan.

I haven't heard from Jasper all day. I know things are too on edge to have Kyra move in straight away, so I told her we would be staying at her place for a couple of days. Her mood matched my own with the news of Hannah. I need to go pack a bag for the night and check in on him.

I come in to loud music—the same stuff from last night. I hear giggling. I knew it wouldn't take him long; God last night was just the start of this torture.

I round the corner to the lounge and feel like I've stepped into a club. He sits on the couch, a blonde and a reddish brunette between his legs; one with his cock in her mouth, and the other rubbing her tits in his thigh. Thank fuck I didn't bring Kyra back here.

He holds a bottle of Jim Beam. "Ohhh, heyyyyy!" he sings when he sees me.

He puts his hand on the back of the brunette's head, pushing her further on to him, his eyes holding mine as he controls her movements. She's slurping like a champ and his eyes hold me hostage. They read a thousand thoughts. They gloss over with pleasure; it's familiar and stirs the attraction inside me.

"Oh fuck!" He turns his head to her, pulls from her mouth and comes all over her chest. She bites her lip while her friend leans in to taste his offering. I want to roar like a beast and slap the shit out of him for proving me right about him always looking for sexual gratification.

"Get dressed and get the fuck out," I command the women. They look up at me, confused.

"Hey, don't be a party pooper, Der. This is Jooge and Michelle. Jooge *is* dressed; she's wearing a pearl necklace from yours truly." He chuckles.

"OUT!" I shout. They scurry to get their clothes on.

"Hey, I only need a minute to suit the joy rider up, and he's ready to go ladies," Jasper calls out as they leave.

"You're drunk, acting like a brat. What if I brought Kyra home to that?"

He hiccups, tipping the bottle to his lips and gulping the contents like it's water. He swipes his mouth. "She'll have to get used to it if she's going to be living here, fucking you. God, I hate you right now."

I move to stand in front of him. "*You* hate *me*? You didn't just come in to witness the porn show."

He throws the bottle across the room. It hits the wall and splinters to the floor. "No, but you crashed into, me left me scattered and fragmented in your wake. I'm trying to put myself back together, but the pieces don't fit anymore. You changed me, awoke me, claimed me, and then broke me. I'm that fucking bottle right now!" He holds his hand to cover his face then lays back. "Just fuck off, Der."

His words impact me like a tornado. All this mess swirling around us, but in the centre of it, it's becoming clear, still, peaceful. He loves me.

Jasper

My head is going to burst and my mouth feels like crap. The light hurts my eyes as I open them and try to adjust to the morning sun. I have a kink in my back from sleeping on the couch.

"You look like shit."

I feel like shit.

I lift my head, despite the pounding making me want to throw up, to answer my dad. "Hey to you, too," I grumble.

"Got to say, Jasp, I never thought I'd see it."

I look over to my father as he sits in the arm chair opposite me. "See what? Me hungover? You've seen it plenty." I moan and lay back, the light making me feel like my eyeballs might burst.

"Love sick."

I scoff. "There's no such thing as love. It's a myth or a disease. It's fucking poison if it's what I'm feeling." I shift so my eyes find his. "This will pass. Love doesn't exist, not for me."

He moves fast, so fast I actually flinch when he appears

two inches from my face.

"That's fucking weak. I didn't raise no weak man. Love takes persistence. It takes courage to open yourself to it, to go after it, embrace and worship it. Your heart beating right now is proof love exists." His finger jabs me in the chest, the look in his eyes reflects the ache in mine. "You were created from a love so fierce, so true that even though your mama has been gone for twenty-eight years, the love still shines bright, here, inside my chest and in yours. It's there in your eyes, your mama's eyes. *You* are that love. Respect the love that created you. Respect that when you find love, it's a gift. Treasure it, feel it, even when it hurts, Jasp. It's what makes us human."

I feel eight not twenty-eight as the tears burn and my jaw quivers. Love makes us weak, but I can't fight what I feel; it's invaded my soul, worked its way into every fibre; every part of me had been touched by it and I want more than anything to have him love me back.

"It hurts, Dad," I manage to say, a stray tear leaking out.

"The best love does, son."

"When did you get here?"

"Just now. I'm not staying. This is a stopover. I met someone; she wants me to meet her folks."

I sit up baffled. "What?"

His laugh brings memories of my childhood. "Yep, she's not your mother, but no one ever will be. But right now someone has claimed a piece of my heart. She's a great women and I want you to meet her when you don't look like someone scraped you off the street."

"Who is she?"

"Her name is Dee, she runs a book shop. She's originally from New Mexico, and she has that tanned skin and dark hair. She's beautiful and good to me."

I feel so elated for him warmth floods my chest, a smile coming for the first time in days. He deserved this and so do I.

* * * * *

He leaves me with the promise of a visit with his new lady friend soon. I go to shower and find Derek on my bed, lost in thought.

"Der?"

"I love you, and so does Ky." He looks at me, his words wrapping me in a cocoon. "It's a fucked up situation, Jasp, and I don't know how to deal with it. What do I do for the best?"

I go to speak, but I'm cut off by his cell ringing. "I need to take this, it's work."

The house phone rings, the machine picking up the call. Sammy's urgent tone has Derek ending his call.

"Der, I can't get your cell. I went to the bathroom and came back to River telling me Kyra left to go get something from her apartment. I don't want to leave her."

Derek grabs the receiver. "I'll send Jasp. We found an address for the suspect. Dawn brought us his stuff and it had a lease in one of his jackets."

He ends the call and grips my shoulders. "Go keep our girl safe, Jasp. I need to go do this. I need to get him."

I see the pain from Mya's death haunt his troubled eyes. "Of course."

* * * * *

"She's not here," I tell him over the phone as I stand staring at Kyra's apartment. My insides are bound so tight I can hardly breathe.

"We have him, Jasp." His voice is a whisper down the line, a tone I've never heard from him. It's almost childlike. It's closure.

"Where is she, then? Do you think he would have done something before you caught him?" I can't stop the fear gathering momentum inside me. I'm happy Derek caught him, but where the fuck is Kyra?

"Have you checked her old apartment? She still has stuff there. I'll meet you at there"

I end the call and rush to the car.

Elation is what I'm feeling when she opens the door. I grab her in a hold so tight I hear the breath whoosh from her lungs. "Fuck, Ky, you scared me, baby."

I lower her to the floor. Tears have gathered in her eyes. "What happened?" I grasp her face in my palms.

"I just needed some space. I can't breathe with everything I'm feeling," she sobs.

"I love you too, Ky." I won't hold back anymore. I let it out, say the words and let them filter in.

"What?"

"I love you."

"And Derek?" she asks, taking me by surprise. "I know you love him, Jasp, but do *you* know?"

Are all the people in my life that perceptive or am I just transparent?

"I know," I breathe. "I know."

I can't resist it any longer. I lower my lips to hers. She tastes so fucking sweet I push her back until she clashes with the wall, my tongue begging for entrance into her mouth as hers flicks out to meet mine. I grab her wrists, pinning them above her head. Her tiny body rubs against mine with a needy intensity. I devour her mouth, my dick straining for release as I grind it against her. Her pants and soft moans are the most delicate, most beautiful sound I've ever heard. I use my free hand to stroke the hardened nipple peaking her dress. I can feel the heat of her pussy against my dick. It wants her tight, warm pussy all around it.

"Thanks for the call to say she's safe." Derek's voice booms into the room.

Kyra gasps against my lips. I rest my forehead on hers, my heavy breathing too hard to control.

"She's safe."

He walks up behind me and moves me from her. She slowly goes to lower her arm, but he stops her. "Don't move, Beauty." He clasps the hem of her dress and lifts it over her head exposing her naked body, all but her pussy on display, and her white cotton panties nearly make me lose it in my jeans.

He grasps under her arms and lifts her around him, her legs winding round his waist, her tits pinned against his chest as his lips find hers. I need to taste her skin. I stroke up her spine, then trace the same path with my lips, her moans fill the room. I reach her neck, my frame and Derek's trapping her between us. Her head rolls to the side to give us access. We both feed from her offering; her skin feels like silk across my tongue. His flicks against mine and I thrust forwards against her ass cheeks which pushes her pussy in to Derek's cock.

"OH, GOD! MORE!" she cries out, making us both groan.

I grip both sides of her panties and tug, snapping the materiel and pulling it free from her. The scent of her arousal assaults my senses in an intoxicating need to have her come undone under my tongue. I drop to my knees, my eyes feast on the glistening pink delights of her pussy. Her pussy is the prettiest pussy—fuck, prettiest anything I'd ever had the honour of seeing. I swipe my tongue to collect the evidence of her lust for us; she tastes like heaven. Pure fucking ecstasy. Her ass jerks against my face, her needy thrusts encouraging me to go on. I dip my tongue into her hot depths and devour every drop she offers.

"Oh God, more."

I fuck her with my tongue, licking, tasting, exploring her heated pink perfection until she's screaming for a release.

"Make her come, Jasp," Derek commands.

I suck her clit into my mouth, sliding two fingers inside her. Her pussy grips me like a vice as I thrust higher, crooking them to stroke her g-spot.

"Oh God …I'm coming …I'm coming," she cries out as her pussy squeezes my fingers; the heated wet release runs down my fingers. I lap it into my mouth before nipping my way up her perfectly toned ass. Derek has her in a deadlock hold as her body trembles and comes back down from the high.

"Kiss me, Jasp. I need to taste her on you."

I comply, encompassing her once again between us, his lips eating away at mine, consuming the essence of her from my tongue. I need inside them so bad.

"Take her."

I grip her, taking her from him. Her warm body wraps around me, her lips pursue a path down my neck. Der strips his clothes off, grabbing my hand and leading us to her bedroom.

I lay her down on the bed, my body moving over her. Her hair splays across the sheets, her hard rose petal nipples tightening as I lick them. I suck one into my mouth and grind my steel cock against her seeping pussy. She is undeniably the most precious being on this earth and she is underneath my body.

Derek's hands stroke up my back, taking my shirt with

them. He lifts it over my head, his mouth tasting the exposed skin.

"Oh God, I ache, please," Kyra begs.

Derek's hands snake around my waist, popping the buttons on my jeans. My hot cock slaps against her abdomen as he tugs my jeans down my legs, tapping my feet to lift them free. The air is a smog of love, lust, and relief. His hands sheath my length with a condom, then line me up against her entrance.

"Oh, fuck," I groan as her tight walls close around the head of my dick.

"Wait for me, Jasp."

"I need more," she pants, her hands reaching round to push my ass cheeks into her. I grab her wrists and pin them above her head.

"Don't be greedy, Ky."

I feel Derek push his sheathed cock against my ass, his hands spreading me, gaining him access to where he wants to be. He pushes inside me, filling me with him and thrusting me forward into her. I hold myself on my forearms, so she's protected from our weight. The atmosphere ignites around us as a chorus of pleasure pleas disturbs the quiet still air. I'm in so deep, her walls cling onto me greedily. Derek's cock thrusts forward, claiming me. The build of the release on the horizon feels like pure euphoria.

Our mixed scents entice more thrusts from me, the sweat clinging and beading our skin, letting us glide effortlessly against each other. I wrap my arms around Kyra's back, cradling her as Derek guides my hips back. I'm in tune with him and know he's changing positions. I hold her to me as he turns us, guiding us so he's lying on the bed with me on top of him, his chest to my back, his cock still buried deep inside me and Kyra still coating my dick in her heat as she adjusts, so she's sitting above us, riding me, her naked form on display for both our eyes to memorise. Her perky, weighted tits move with a natural mesmerising bounce as she thrusts and twists her hips.

It's incredible, the silky warmth coating me, gliding over me, contracting and sucking at me for a release. Derek is so deep, pushing his hips into me, his teeth biting down on my shoulder. I reach up to cup her tits, feel them in my hands. She throws her head back, her movements more erratic as she tightens over me.

"OH, GOD YES…JASPER… DEREK! YES, I'M COMING!"

"FUCCKKKK!" We roar in unison as I flood her with my release and Derek floods me with his. Her come coats my dick and trickles out onto my balls, her body collapsing over me.

I cradle her to my chest. Kissing her head, I shift, so we can move our weight from Derek. He rolls to his side facing us, his hand tracing her bare back, his lips nibbling my shoulder.

"I love you," he breathes.

I love you too," I tell him.

"I love you both," Kyra mumbles, exhausted in a dreamy voice, making Derek's chest vibrate with a laugh and mine rock her with my chuckle.

We let sleep claim us.

* * * * *

I'm content. So happy and vibrating with love. I have Kyra between me and Derek, sated from our love making. We woke and made love multiple times throughout the night.

The early morning sun cast a yellow sheen over them; I'm in heaven right now.

"I need to go to work." Derek's groggy voice skims over Kyra to my ears. I enjoy the show as he gets up, his naked body hard and muscular. I will never get enough. I watch him dress. He leans down to kiss my lips, then Kyra's head. "See you both tonight at our house."

* * * * *

I love watching Kyra dance. She's breathtaking and I feel myself fall deeper into her every damn time I watch her. She's an effortless beauty.

My cell rings, shrilling throughout the studio where just Kyra, Amy—a student here preparing for an audition to get into a school— and I are. I look at the incoming video message and it takes me a few minutes to realise what I'm seeing. It's River, her blonde hair swaying as she rushes to her car. Someone's videoing her. The image shuffles around and then the back of her car comes into view through a windshield as if someone is following her and filming at the same time.

Every nerve inside me goes taut, the nightmares from my dreams manifest into the present, coating me in their dark dread. I snap the phone shut and walk outside while dialing her number. Each ring takes years off my life.

Ring……………ring ………………..ring

"Jasp, baby, I'm late for an appointment. Can I ring you back?"

A wash of relief passes through me until I hear cars and realise she's driving, and they could still be following her.

"River, listen, I need you to forget the appointment and drive to Derek at the station, do you hear me? I'll phone him and get him to meet you outside. Do not get out of your car." I enforce.

"What's happening, Jasp?" The strength in her voice makes me love her even more. She is so strong.

"Please River, do this for me. Please?"

"Okay, I'll leave again. I just pulled in."

I hear her horn blast. "Hey move, asshole, you're blocking me in!" she shouts. "What the fuck? Sorry, Jasp, some asshole is blocking me in and getting out of his truck."

"Where are you, River?"

"The grave site car park. MOVE YOUR TRUCK!" she shouts.

I hear a muffled noise, then nothing. I've only felt this scared once before, when Danny was letting me die at his feet. I'm so scared that my blood turns cold and my soul leaves my body for a few minutes.

I rush to my car, my mind static. I drive on auto pilot and I notice nothing around me; I'm numb.

I pull in to the grave site and see Derek's car and River's blonde hair peeking through his arms as he holds her close to him. I leap from the car.

"River?"

"I'm fine, Jasp," she assures me, coming into my open arms. I feel my heartbeat pounding from my chest. She's okay. She's here, fine in my arms, I reassure myself.

"Where's Kyra?" Derek asks, looking behind me into my car.

"At the studio. Shit, I didn't even tell her I was leaving."

Derek's eyes flash with something I've never seen there before: fear. River's body has gone solid still in my embrace. I watch Derek as he puts his phone to his ear. "Get River in your car, we can come back for hers."

We rush to my car and follow Derek to the studio, River

ringing Kyra's cell and Amy's. "Nothing," she breathes.

Despair sets into my stomach, consuming the euphoria of the night and morning. The helplessness is like a physical pain tearing my insides to shreds.

We pull up and jump from the car, Derek a few feet ahead of us. The bell chimes overhead as we open the front door; the music is still playing, but there's no noise from movement. My heart stops when I see blood. So much blood.

My head fills with visions of myself bleeding out in River's back yard, then the pale frame of Amy's lifeless body fills my sight. Her eyes hold no light as they stare wide open at nothing. Eighteen years old and she's gone. The gash across her throat seeps a river of red all around her.

Derek drops beside her to check her pulse, but it's pointless.

"Get River out of here, Jasp. Now."

I will my legs to unlock from the stiff stance they hold me in, and my eyes find the tear-soaked face of River. Pain, so much pain written in her beautiful features. I reach my hand out and grasp hers, pulling her along with me as I hurry us from the studio.

I don't see it, but I feel the impact when something hits me in the head.

Kyra

I watch out of the window as Jasper takes off. He looks pale and worried as he drives from the parking lot.

"Get some water, Amy. You're doing great, you're going to kill this audition."

I smile over at her, but the smile slips when I see man coming up behind her with a purposeful pace. I feel like I fell asleep; this can't be real. This isn't happening. I try to convince myself as Amy's eyes go wide, and then confusion, shock, and sorrow flits through them before she reaches up to the hand that's just sliced her neck open. Red liquid life pours from her, staining her skin. I want to scream. I want to save her... I want to wake up.

Please, please let me wake up. A choked sob wrenches from my body as hers falls with a sickening thud. How can this be happening? How can she be dancing, beaming with life and light, and now a few minutes later, be lying in a crimson river?

I watch as he walks towards me: blonde messy hair, green eyes, chiselled features. He's so handsome. I know I should run. I know I should try to escape, fight, scream, but all I can think about is this must be a dream, this must be a dream. He'll

get to me and I'll wake, I'll wake up, I'll wake up.
    I didn't.

Derek

I felt a shift in the air today. Something was different; it wasn't just the fact my every wish and desire was fulfilled last night, it was something else. I dreamed of Mya last night; she was trying to tell me something. She was on the cliff top, pointing and shaking her head. I woke with a panic, but it was quickly washed away when Kyra's small hand stroked my cheek.

"Bad dream," she whispered as her scent filled my senses. We had come a long way. Her touch soon aroused me and we made love again, clearing the dream from my thoughts.

I had to go into the precinct, so I could watch as they questioned him. I needed answers. When I got to his apartment and they were already bringing him out, I felt cheated. I wanted to kill him, but at the very least get the arrest. He sneered at me, but I felt nothing but relief that we had him. We finally had him.

I went to the office, but my thoughts were on Kyra. She had a dance practice at the studio, and Jasper was taking her. I just couldn't remove the sinking feeling from the pit of my stomach, and then I received the news that Evan had been released, they couldn't hold him—no evidence. He had a lawyer come in and have him out in the early hours of this morning. Then a letter arrived, changing everything I had believed for ten long painful years. Years that had taken a toll on my soul. Guilt wears on you. It never leaves me and this letter intensified that guilt.

Derek,

My brother will support me and protect me and my child.
Those were your sister's last words before I seized her cell from her grasp that she was going to use to call you. Her balance was never the best and she fell backwards. The look on her face as her hand reached down to cradle my baby growing in her womb. Shock, fear, hurt.

You killed her.

Convincing her she didn't need ME.
She belonged to ME.
That baby was made by ME.
You'll learn my pain when you watch the ones you love die.
I'll start with that delicious blonde you seem so fond of.

I immediately locate River through the GPS on her cell; she was going to the cemetery. She always went on a Saturday. Her phone was just a busy tone and I kept redialling while driving to her. I had to brake hard when a truck came barrelling out of the parking gate. The hairs on the back of my neck stood on end when I saw her petite frame standing with her hands on her hips and a glare on her face. I almost chuckled at her fierce pose. She was okay. I jumped from the car and ran to her; she didn't seem surprised to see me and welcomed my embrace without question.

"What's happening? That guy came right up to me and gave me this.

Always promising to protect, but you didn't before and won't again.

Jasper's truck screeched to a stop and he looked ill as he grabbed River from me, holding her and breathing hard.

* * * * *

I have never felt true fear before. I've felt nervous, confused, heartbroken, soul crippling grief, but never true fear, even after being shot. I have never felt anything like the dark monster that consumes me in this moment. Blood, dark red and draining from a girl who had been bright, beautiful and talented; a daughter, sister, friend, is now lifeless and gone; a memory that will haunt the people who love her every day.

I can't bear to see her like this. I look up at River, a woman I adored who had witnessed hell and pulled herself from it, and here she is, seeing true horror once again.

"Get River out of here, Jasp. Now."

I pull my phone and ring for back up. I hear a muffled noise; reaching for my gun, I follow the sound to see River outside the studio main door. She's on the ground. "Riv?"

I look around, my eyes darting to a pick-up truck different to the one at the cemetery.

"Go, Derek. He took Jasp."

"I'm not leaving you."

Sirens pierce the air.

"The police are almost here. Go, Derek. Don't let him take my family."

I rush to my car. My cell rings and I put the hands free on as I screech from the studio and speed to keep up with the truck.

"Follow me, Derek. You call me in and I see any sign of the cops, I drive us off the cliff." The call ends.

I lose him in the traffic, but drive to the cliff top.

All my old feelings about this place are transformed now I see it knowing he killed my baby sister. She didn't take her life. She was going to come to me.

My guts clench as I roll to a stop. Kyra and Jasper stand near the cliff's edge. Evan holds a gun on them; old demons haunt Jasper's features. He's ghost white. Kyra cries, blood staining her lips. The fucker hit her.

I step out of the car cautiously.

"Gun. Throw it over."

I toss my gun at his feet. "This isn't about them, let them go."

His callous laugh sends shiver through me. "This all about them. You love them. I watched you a lot and you're such a confident, self-involved prick you didn't think I would be so close, watching everything you do. Who knew you had a thing for dick? That's probably why you made her leave me, because you wanted me."

I growl and step towards him.

"Uh, uh." He waves the gun at them and a sob tears from Kyra. "So, eeny, meeny, miney, mo."

I hear the shot crack the air like a thunder bolt. Life slows. I run at him, tackling to the ground. Kyra's screams kill my soul as she calls out Jasper's name.

This can't be real.

I punch Evan hard, feeling his cheek crumble under my fist. His gun falls over the edge. I wrap my hands around his neck and squeeze. His eyes flare, and the veins pop as I tighten the grip. His knee comes up hard against my balls, forcing me to release my hold as he tackles and wrestles me. I land a few more blows. One to the temple, knocking him out. I search for my gun, crawling to retrieve it. I pick it up and stand.

"Derek!" Kyra screams. I turn and fire a round into his chest, the force staggering him backwards. He looks down at the red holes painting his shirt; his shocked face lifts to me.

I step forward and kick the son of a bitch over the ledge.

Kyra

It was a year ago today since that awful day when Evan changed me. Dark people are everywhere, but it's the light that overcomes it all that wins in the end.

"This is your uncle," I tell Mya, looking down at the grave as she gurgles. My heart constricts as Derek's hands come around my waist.

"You okay?" I hand the baby to River.

"It's just so tragic," I whisper to him, burrowing my face in his neck.

River lays the flowers and swipes her grief from her face. "I still miss him every day." She smiles. "He was my brother."

I look down at her brother's grave, then next to it where Derek had a headstone placed for Mya. Jasper's hand moves to my back, his kisses welcome as they touch my head.

The bullet scratched his shoulder that day, a flesh wound. When Derek got closure and vengeance for his sister, I felt lighter for him.

He rushed over, fear transforming his features, and dropped to his knees. "Oh God, Jasp. Where are you hit?"

Derek followed my hand to the small bloody stain on his

shoulder and broke into tears. "I thought he killed you. I can't fucking breathe," Derek choked out.

"Yes, you can. None of us are going anywhere. You fucking own my heart. I refuse to let it stop beating," Jasper replied.

And he didn't. We've been inseparable ever since. We're made up of broken parts, and we all loved the broken parts of us.

The End

About the Author

When not lost in her mind of characters Ker can be found reading or spending time with family.

She has a passion for music, attending concerts with her sister and enjoying the occasional nights out with girlfriends.

She can also be found having in-depth chats about book boyfriends on face book in some amazing groups and blogs.

For news, updates and teasers come join me on Facebook
Author Facebook Page
Email here at
kerryduke34@gmail.com

Add me on Goodreads
The Broken Goodreads

The Broken is available now
Amazon
Amazon.co.uk

Acknowledgements

Where to begin, Ing, from As the Pages Turn, for hosting my blog tour, thank you!!! Jooge for arranging my Blitz and just being awesome I love you!. All my Kinky Kittens street team you are all great but an extra thanks to my hard-core pimp-ers, Jacy, Terrie, Michelle, colleen, Kelly, Kristin, Jade, Sarah, Robyn, Rhonda. You have all become friends, I love you guys.

To every blog that promoted, featured, had me takeover. You guys are just amazing support thank you!

To all my fellow authors who support me and one another, you guys rock!

Thank you to Pepper Winters, as always a fantastic support and friend. Another awesome friend from down under, Rachel Brookes for our late night/ morning chats. Vicki Leaf, Vikki Ryan awesome betas and friends. Nikki Blissfulblog huge support and friend, "you and me baby". Zack Love for applying his anal perfectionism to my book blurb and for his friendship.

Dawn Stancil aka D.H Sidebottem where to begin, I love you hard woman, you kept me from drowning the last weeks from release. You're an amazing writer and invaluable friend to me.

Kim, Claire and everyone from my admin in our Fictional group and page! Jade from BFF! Leah my beautiful supportive sister. Family and friends who I neglect to hide in my cave. Thank you to my amazing editor, Kyra who let me pinch her name and skills thank you, it's awesome to have an editor who comments on an edit with "LOL" at your funny scenes, hehe! Jade and team at Black firefly, Michelle from Alexandmedesign. For an incredible cover thank you! You can find her amazing work here https://www.facebook.com/pages/Alex-me-design/190567480986754?ref=br_tf

Most of all thank you the passionate readers I adore you all <3

Keep reading for a look at what's coming next from Author Ker Dukey

***

MY SOUL KEEPER
A paranormal romance coming soon
❖❖❖

What if your entire reality changed on you one day? You wake up and your family and friends aren't who you thought they were. You look around, and the world isn't what you thought it was. You don't even recognize yourself. You and your reality are a complete mystery to you.

Simone's life was about to undergo that disturbing journey.

Love, lust, death, betrayal.

How do you fight the devil himself when he consumes you with lust?

How can you love someone who has come to take back your brother's soul?

Shamar, soul keeper and son of Death, had never met such a unique soul before Simone. Captivated by her, he broke all rules to be near her -- to love and protect her

But how do you protect someone from evil when the forces of good seem to be working against you?

When Lucifer himself crawled from Hell to claim Simone, what sacrifices would Shamar make to keep her safe?

Printed in Great Britain
by Amazon.co.uk, Ltd.,
Marston Gate.